DELPHINE DE VIG[...] [...] bestselling *No and Me*, [...] in Britain, *Nothing Hol[...] [...]k the Night, Underground Time, Based on a True Story* and *Loyalties*. She lives in Paris.

GEORGE MILLER is the translator into English of all four of Delphine de Vigan's titles. He is also a regular translator for *Le Monde diplomatique*'s English-language edition.

We laugh, we drink. And in us the wounded,
The hurt go by; we owe them memory and life. For living
Is knowing that every instant of life is a golden sunbeam
On a sea of darkness, it's knowing how to say thank you.

FRANÇOIS CHENG, *Enfin le royaume*

Where do the words go?
The words that resist,
Withdraw,
The ones that argue
And poison [...]
Where do the words go?
The ones that make and unmake us,
That save us
When all else goes.

LA GRANDE SOPHIE

MARIE

Have you ever wondered how many times a day you say thank you? Thank you for the salt, for holding the door, for the information.

Thanks for the change, for the bread, for that packet of cigarettes.

Thank yous out of politeness, social convention – automatic and mechanical. Almost meaningless.

Sometimes omitted.

Sometimes over-emphasised: *thank* you. Thanks for everything. Thanks a million.

Many thanks.

Professional thank yous: thank you for your response, your attention, your participation.

————

Have you ever wondered how many times in your life you've *really* said thank you? A genuine thank you. Expressed your gratitude, your recognition, your debt?

And to whom?

The teacher who turned you on to books? The young man who stepped in the day you were mugged in the street? The doctor who saved your life?

Life itself?

Today an old lady I loved died.

I often used to say, 'I owe her a huge amount.' And: 'But for her, I mightn't be here.'

I'd say, 'She matters a lot to me.'

Mattering, owing – is that how gratitude is measured?

Did I thank her enough? Did I show my gratitude enough?

Was I close enough, present enough, constant enough?

And I'm thinking about the last few months, the last few hours.

Our conversations and smiles and silences.

Shared moments come back to me. Others have vanished. And the moments I missed can be invented.

I'm trying to remember the day when I grasped that a major change had occurred and our remaining time together was now counted.

It happened suddenly. From one day to the next.

I don't mean it came completely out of the blue. Sometimes Michka would stop in the middle of her living room, disorientated, as though she no longer knew where to begin, as if the ritual, though she'd performed it many times before, suddenly eluded her. Other times, she'd stop in the middle of a sentence, almost literally bumping up against something invisible. She'd look for one word but come up with another. Or else would draw a complete blank, like encountering a trap that she had to get around. But for the whole of that time, she lived alone, in her own home. Independent. And she kept reading, watching television, receiving visitors now and then.

And then that autumn day that arrived unannounced . . .

Before then, she'd coped. Afterwards, she didn't.

I can picture her in her apartment with its low ceilings, on her own, sitting in her armchair. Behind her the curtains are drawn, but there's a hint of afternoon light through a chink. The paint on the walls has yellowed a bit. The furniture, the pictures, the ornaments on the shelves, everything around her seems to come from a time long ago.

Her name's Michka. She's an old woman who seems like a young girl. Or a young girl who's become old by accident, the victim of some malign fate. Her long, knotty hands are gripping the arms of her chair as though she's in danger of capsizing.

Suddenly a series of beeps breaks the silence. Michka seems surprised, looks around and notices the bracelet on her wrist as though the noise might be coming from this strange, ugly object that she was reluctantly persuaded to wear.

Then the voice of the helpline operator comes through.

'Hello, Mrs Seld, this is Muriel from the helpline. Did you press your alarm?'

'Yes.'

'Have you had a fall?'

'No, no.'

'Do you feel unwell?'

'Not really.'

'Can you tell me what's the matter?'

'I'm afraid.'

'Can you tell me where you are, Mrs Seld?'

'In the living room.'

'Are you hurt?'

'No, but . . . I'm starting to lose . . .'

'You've lost something?'

Michka clings on tighter, feeling as though the armchair is pitching beneath her, or maybe it's the floor that's giving way. She doesn't reply.

'Are you sitting down?'

'Yes, I'm in my armchair. But I can't move.'

'You can't get up?'

'No.'

'How long have you been sitting there, Mrs Seld?'

'I don't know. Since this morning, I think. I sat down after breakfast as musual, to do my crossword. But I couldn't do any of it. And then, I . . . I wanted . . . I couldn't get up . . . I'm losing everything, that's why.'

'What have you lost, Mrs Seld?'

'It's not visible. But I can feel it. It's excaping . . . escaping.'

'Can you move your legs, Mrs Seld?'

'No, no, no. I can't. It's all over. I'm scared.'

'You really can't get up?'

'No.'

'Have you had lunch today?'

'Not really.'

'So you've been in your chair since this morning and haven't moved?'

'Yes, that's right.'

'I'm going to call one of the people on your contact list, is that all right?'

'Yes.'

I'm sure Michk' heard the quick tap of the woman's fingers on her keyboard.

'I have the name of a Miss Marie Chapier. Shall I call her?'

'I don't know . . .'

'Is she your daughter?'

'No.'

'Do you want me to call her?'

'Yes, please. Tell her I didn't want to . . . truffle her, but it's because I'm losing something, something important.'

Muzak replaces the operator's voice. Michka remains still, looking straight ahead in a state of focused expectation that I'm familiar with. A few seconds later, the operator returns.

'Mrs Seld, are you still there?'

'Yes.'

'Marie's coming round right away. She says she'll be there in twenty, twenty-five minutes. She'll let your doctor know.'

'All night.'

She says 'all night' in exactly the tone you would say 'all right'.

'All night what?'

'Yes, all night.'

'I'm not far away, Mrs Seld. I'm going to get on with my work, but if you don't feel well, press the button on your bracelet again and I'll be here, OK?'

'Yes, all night. Thank you.'

Michka remains in her chair, arms on the armrests. She tries to steady her breathing.

She closes her eyes.

A few moments later, she hears a little girl's voice.

Am I going to sleep at yours? Will you leave the light on? Will you stay here? Can you leave the door open? Will you stay with me?

She smiles. The little girl's voice is a memory that's both pleasant and painful.

Can we have breakfast together? Are you scared? Do you know where my school is? Don't put the light out, OK? Will you take me if Mummy can't?

I gave the bell a quick press and immediately put the key in the lock.

I went into the room and there she was, clinging on to her chair as though it had been carried off on the tide.

I went over and gave her a kiss. I smelled the sweet smell of her hairspray, which still conjures up memories as powerfully as ever.

'Hey, Michk', what's going on?'

'I don't know. I'm afraid.'

'I'll help you get up, OK?'

'No, no, no.'

'But Michk', when I was here three days ago you were walking fine with your stick. I'm sure you can get up.'

I put my arm around her to help her. She leaned on the armrests to give herself purchase. She got to her feet, looking surprised. She was a bit shaky, but managed to stay upright.

'You see!'

'Did I tell you I fell in the living room?'

'Yes, Michka, you told me.'

'Head over wheels.'

I handed her her stick and then went round her other side so she could take my arm.

'Right, off we go!'

'Careful, eh . . .'

'You must be starving . . .'

We went towards the kitchen. She was hanging on to me, taking tiny steps forward. Gradually, I sensed she was regaining her confidence.

'Could be worst . . .'

But from that day on, Michka couldn't live alone any more.

Michka's sitting in front of a desk piled with files in a nondescript room. The big black leather chair on the other side is empty.

She's singing to herself as if for reassurance.

I'm a brave little soldier
I must be bold and strong
A brave little soldier
And I must carry on
I'm a brave little soldier

A severe-looking woman comes into the room. She's carrying a giant file, which she slams down on the desk. Unsmiling, she looks at Michka. She has huge finger-nails, painted a dark colour. She sits down in her chair and says coldly, 'Can you introduce yourself, Mrs Seld?'

Michka immediately feels intimidated.

'Well . . . My name is Michèle Seld, but people call me Michka.'

'Good. Are you married?'

'No.'

'Do you have children?'

'No.'

The director lets the silence linger. She's waiting for details.

'I . . . I travelled a lot with my work. I was a photo-journalist for magazines. And later I was a proofreader for a newspaper. I read through the articles. Nothing got past me: typos, bad grammar, the wrong verb, repetition—'

The director interrupts.

'Why do you want to leave your current position?'

Michka doesn't understand the question. She's unable to hide a flash of panic on her face. She looks around for someone who could help, but she's all alone with this woman who's drumming impatiently on the desk because she's slow to reply. The director's nails make a dull grating sound on the formica.

'Well . . . I have to tell you that I've been retired a long time . . .'

The woman gives a forced smile that's hard to interpret. Then sighs ostentatiously.

'Let me phrase the question differently, Mrs Seld. What was it that caused your interest in our establishment?'

'Perhaps I got the wrong room . . . I mean, office . . .
I didn't know you had to go through this, I mean, that
you had to do this.'

The director is no longer concealing her exasperation.

'Mrs Seld, you are having an admission interview for
a place in a nursing home.' (As she goes on, her tone
becomes increasingly brusque.) 'You need to show the
best of yourself because, need I remind you, we receive
countless applications.'

'No, no . . . of course. I understand. But I didn't
prepare anything. I didn't know you had to have an
admission interview.'

The woman loses her temper.

'So what *did* you think, Mrs Seld? That we took
in anyone at all, just like that? What an idea! There
isn't enough space for everyone, as you very well
know. Not enough space! It's the same with everything – whatever you do, you have to have tests,
interviews, competitions, exams, assessments, evalu-
ations, grading! You have to show your dedication,
your commitment, your motivation, your determin-
ation! At school, at university, at work, everywhere,
Mrs Seld, yes, everywhere – *e-ve-ry-where* – we have
to grade, sift, select! We have no choice. Sort the
wheat from the chaff, even in a nursing home. It's
the way of the world. I don't make the rules, I just
apply them.'

This seems to make an impression on Michka.

'You mean you have to prove yourself.'

'Exactly. What are your strong points, what's your greatest weakness, what are your strategies for improvement, what's your capacity for development? How can you be your best self?'

'I'm an old lady, you know.'

'And that's the problem, Mrs Seld.'

'And I . . . I can no longer remain at home. I'm afraid . . . I lose things . . . I'm afraid it's getting worse.'

The woman sighs again. Melodramatically.

'You're not making this easy for me. Can you dance at least?'

'Yes, a bit.'

'Show me.'

Michka gets up. Walking hesitantly at first, she moves back from the desk. Then she begins to dance, her movements like those of a little girl. She pirouettes, her arms joined above her head. She rises on her toes; she's graceful. Gradually her body becomes more supple; she enters into it and dances better and better, her gestures become freer. She smiles.

She now resembles a young girl. Her movements are precise and controlled. She's beaming.

The woman notes something in her file. Then, without a word, gets up and leaves the room.

———

Michka remains alone in the centre of a circle of light, still dancing for herself.

Then she moves into the shadows and disappears.

She recounted her dreams to me several times. There were variations. Either because the memory of them was gradually becoming sharper, or because she was adding details she thought more striking, so that we – we who came and went freely, we who were in full possession of our faculties – could grasp the feeling of terror that was dragging her under.

The day of the appointment has come. Michka's sitting in the same place as in her dream. But I'm there beside her.

Both of us facing the desk, waiting for the director. Michka's tense, as though she's about to take an important oral exam.

'Don't worry, Michk', it'll be fine. It's just so they can get to know you.'

'Are you sure I don't have to have an investigation . . . interview . . . prove myself . . . to get in?'

'No, no. You'll see.'

I look at her and smile. Her face seems to relax a little. She takes the opportunity to look at me with mock confusion.

'Have you had your hair done?'

'Yes, Michk', I've had it done.'

A woman comes into the office. She looks kind and affable. She's wearing a light suit.

She puts a file down in front of her.

She speaks to Michka.

'If I understand correctly, Mrs Seld, you were living independently until a few weeks ago?'

Michka nods cautiously. She's on guard.

'But now you can no longer remain alone . . . According to your doctor, you've had several falls in the past few months, one of which required a short spell in hospital. You suffer from vertigo, which partly explains your fears and your difficulty moving around at home.'

Michka makes a small movement of her chin in agreement. The lady is still scanning the file.

'Do you get out?'

'A little, with Marie. Once a week. I used to do laps of the balcony at home, but I can't do that any more.'

'Laps of the balcony?'

'Yes, round and round, like a crinimal . . . ten circuits, sometimes even twenty, when I was in shape. It's ten steps across, then two steps up, that makes twelve. I'll let you tut it up.'

The director is watching Michka, trying to work out to what extent she's sending herself up. But she's not. Michka is proud: 120 steps a day is an achievement.

She looks at me as though she's passing the baton; it's over to me.

'When I go round, we always try to have a walk outdoors, but Michka's increasingly afraid because of her falls, and because of everything going on around her. Things move too fast for her: children, people in a rush.'

'Have you thought about caring for her at home?'

'Yes, of course. But the problem is having someone there day and night. Michka can't be by herself at all. She's afraid.'

Michka adds: 'At night, there are . . . nightmares.'

'I thought about her moving in with me, but she won't hear of it.'

'Oh no, it's on the sixth floor and there's no clift and anyway, there's no reason why Marie should look after me!'

The director turns to me enquiringly. But I look at Michka and want her to meet my eye. I wait for her watery gaze to look up and focus on my face.

'Of course there is, Michk'! There are lots of reasons.'

'No, out of the question. Old people are a burton. It wouldn't work. I'm well aware how these things burn out, believe me.'

The director looks at us both, then says to me: 'So for the moment, you've moved in with Mrs Seld?'

'Yes, at night I have. I've found someone who can take over while I'm at work during the day.'

'I shall call you when a place becomes available. We're in touch with the doctor, who endorsed the application.

It could happen quickly, but I can't give you a precise date. It depends on . . . departures.'

The director gets up. Michka looks at me, waiting for my signal. I help her to her feet and pick up her stick.
Taking little steps, we leave the room.

She pulls the door of her apartment behind her, the door she's closed hundreds of times before. But today she knows it's the last time. She wants to lock the door herself. She knows she won't be back. She'll never again perform the routine she's gone through hundreds of times before: turning on the television, smoothing down the bedspread, washing the saucepan, lowering the shutters because of the sun, hanging her dressing gown on the hook in the bathroom, plumping up the sofa cushions to try to restore the shape they lost long ago. She's given away the furniture, the bed, the video player, the pans and the toaster. She's kept a few books, the photo albums, about thirty letters and the official documents she's obliged to retain. But in reality she knows she's leaving everything behind.

Michka has just moved in to her new room. The furniture's simple: a bed and bedside table, a chair, a desk, a cupboard. Formica, plastic and light wood. Soft pastel tones. Decent quality. She sits down in the only armchair while I finish putting her things away. She's looking around at the clean, bare walls and the floral curtains. I can see she's scowling. She's in a gloomy mood.

'Don't worry, you can decorate. We'll hang some pictures on the walls and put a nice pot plant on the table.'

'What for?'

'To make it more welcoming.'

'We're not going to pretend I'm at home, though.'

'No, we're not, Michk', but that's no reason for it to be sad. You'll be staying here a good while, all the same.'

'Yes, well, we'll see.'

(I don't know if she's alluding to the impermanence of this home or a more definitive departure.) She got out of bed the wrong side. Suddenly, her expression brightens.

'Did you find my bottle in the bag?'

'Which bottle?'

'My whisky.'

'Yes, yes, it's there. But maybe it's not such a good idea, Michk', after the falls you've had . . . Are you sure you want to keep it?'

'Oh, listen, I have a little thumbleful in the evening from a tiny glass. That won't kill me. Will you put it in the hanger for me? Not too high and not too low, behind the clothes, please, that would be great.'

'Are you sure it's allowed?'

'Not so much as such. But that doesn't worry me. This isn't the army, after all.'

I take out the bottle I'd deliberately left in the bag and put it in the cupboard, following her instructions as closely as possible.

'Not so high! There, just below. Behind the wool-overs . . . the pullovers. There, that's it.'

Instantly she seems happy.

I sit down on the chair beside her while she leafs through the welcome booklet. I know her; she's looking for something to grumble about.

'Lunch, twelve o'clock. Afternoon tea, four. Dinner, half six. This is the high life, eh!'

I smile.

'They look old, don't you think? Did you see them, those women in the day room, in those chairs with . . . wheels. They're well past the third age.'

'I don't know, Michk'. There are probably big differences between them. People are here for different reasons. You're not one of the oldest.'

'Really?' (She seems reassured.) 'You know, it feels odd all the same.'

'I can imagine, Michk'.'

That's not true. I can't imagine any of it. Because it's unimaginable. I put my hand on her arm. I try to think of something to say, something that will comfort her – 'Those ladies are nice' or 'I'm sure you'll make friends' or 'There are lots of activities' – but each of these phrases would be an insult to the woman she used to be.

So I say nothing.

I simply remain by her side.

She lies down on the bed and nods off.

A few minutes later a woman comes into the room to offer her a snack. A *nice little* carton of apple juice with a *nice little* straw, and a *nice little* cake wrapped in a *nice little* sachet. Like in a day centre.

So this is what lies ahead for you, Michk': little steps, little naps, little teas, little trips, little visits.

A shrunken, diminished life, but a perfectly ordered one.

I try to phone more often.

But it's harder on the phone. She has trouble hearing and quickly becomes confused. So, try as I might, conversation dwindles, becomes formulaic, dries up. Her voice suddenly seems so far away. I try my best, but it's no use. I always end up talking to her as if she were a child and that breaks my heart, because I know what kind of woman she was. I know she's read Doris Lessing, Sylvia Plath and Virginia Woolf, that she's kept her subscription to *Le Monde* and still goes through the whole paper every day, though now she only scans the headlines.

But I say: Did you sleep well? Are you eating well? Is everything OK? Have you been able to read a bit? Have you been watching television? Have you made friends? Have you stayed in your room? Haven't you been to the film club?

Instead of saying, give me some peace, why don't you go out and drink my health and get up on the table and dance, she replies politely to every one of my questions. She makes an effort, searches for the right words.

When I hang up, I'm overwhelmed by a sense of my powerlessness and unable to speak.

JÉRÔME

I knocked several times, but she can't have heard me.

She's alone in her room.

She's looking for something.

She opens the cupboard several times, then the desk drawers. She picks up the magazines on her bedside table. She seems disorientated. She keeps repeating the same sequence: cupboard, drawers, beside table. She looks around, trying to decide where to try next.

Suddenly she puts her stick on the bed and leans on the mattress to get down on her knees. She wants to look under the bed. This position seems painful, so she lies flat on her stomach with her head under the bed.

This is how I meet her for the first time.

'Hello, Mrs Seld. I'm Jérôme, the speech therapist.'

She almost bumps her head on the underside of the bed. I go over to help her up.

'Let me help.'

It's not easy, given the challenging position she's got herself into, half of her body under the bed and the other half out.

'Stay on the floor, Mrs Seld. Yes, like that. Your arms too. And if I may, I'm going to pull you towards me a little bit so that you can get up. Don't move . . . Careful, I'll pull a little . . . There you are . . . Careful . . . Don't raise your head . . . I'm pulling a bit more. There, that's it!'

With difficulty, and still on the floor, she rolls on to her side so she can see me.

'Ah, hello.'

She shakes my hand as though this were all perfectly normal: her, stretched out on the lino, unable to get up by herself, and me, crouching beside her. In a split second, eyes darting, she sizes me up.

I help her sit up and then get to her feet. This takes time. Her movements are careful, as are mine.

She motions to me to pass her stick, which I do.

Then she smiles with a hint of guilt.

'Call me Michka.'

'With pleasure.'

'"Mrs Seld this and Mrs Seld that . . ." It's sad living among people who don't call you by your first name, you know.'

I'm surprised by her sparkiness.

'I understand. I promise I'll call you Michka. Were you looking for something?'

'Yes, because . . . I lose a lot . . . It's happening quickly. I feel nearly all the time that I'm losing, but I don't know what and . . . that frightens me. I'd like to say more but . . . no can't do, you understand?'

'I saw from your file that you're suffering from the onset of aphasia. The doctor will have explained that that means you have trouble finding your words. Sometimes they don't come at all and sometimes you replace them with others. It depends on the situation, how you're feeling, whether you're tired . . .'

'I see. If you say so.'

'Perhaps it was words you were looking for, Michka?'

'Yes, fossibly.'

'I'm a speech therapist. Do you know what that is?'

'Oh, yes. I used to be a proofreader in a big . . . house. For years.'

'Great. We're going to work really well together, you'll see. We'll do exercises, puzzles, things like that.'

She's observing me. Without embarrassment, she examines me from head to toe and back again, as though deciding then and there whether or not to add me to her schedule. And then she decides, in exactly the tone she'd use to say 'Of course':

'Off course.'

I can't help laughing, and then she laughs too. For a few seconds we laugh just for the pleasure of laughing.

Then the laughter stops.

'Where does it happen?'

'What's that?'

'The games.'

'They happen in your room, Mrs . . . Michka. I'll come a couple of times a week, on Tuesdays and Thursdays.'

'Ah, in my room, that's fine.'

For a few seconds she's thoughtful.

'Have I told you I have nightmares?'

'No, you haven't told me that.'

'Can I tell you about them when you come?'

'Yes, of course. So I'll see you tomorrow then? Tomorrow's Tuesday.'

'Yes, that's fine.'

When I meet them for the first time, I'm always looking for the same thing, an image of the person they used to be. Behind the blurred vision and uncertain movements, the stooped or bent posture, as though trying to make out an original sketch beneath an ugly felt-pen drawing, I look for the young man or woman they once were. I look at them and think: he or she too once loved, shouted, enjoyed sex or plunging into water, ran until they were out of breath, climbed stairs four at a time, danced the night away. She or he too caught trains, took the metro, went on country walks or to the mountains, drank wine, slept in, talked nineteen to the dozen. These thoughts move me. I can't stop myself hunting for that image, trying to bring it back to life.

I like seeing photos in which they're looking into the lens with no inkling of the losses they'd suffer – or in which that idea was still purely theoretical – in which they stood up straight with no need of support. I like seeing them in the prime of life – but what age is the prime? Twenty? Thirty? Forty?

Sometimes it's impossible to make the connection between the young man or woman in the photo and the person in front of me. Even with the greatest acuity, the greatest discernment, nothing seems to link those two bodies: the light, self-confident body of youth and the deformed, diminished body in the nursing home.

I look at the photos and say, 'It looks just like you, Mrs Ermont!' or, 'What a handsome man you were, Mr Terdian!'

In the early days, a voice in my head would cry out, 'But what happened then? How is it possible? Is this really what awaits us all, without exception? Is there no way around, no fork in the road, no alternative route that would make it possible to escape this calamity?'

In the early days, I worked with different groups: children, adults, the elderly. Then gradually the bulk of my time came to be focused on old people's homes. I can't claim it was a decision or a choice. It just happened. Opportunities. And a sort of inevitability. Now I split my time among several institutions. I have my sector.

I'm fine with it. It's where I belong.

———

I like watching them, seeing how they fight it every step of the way.

I like their voices, which feel their way, tremulous and hesitant.

I admit that I record them. Not all of them, just some. From the first session. I have a tiny digital recorder with dozens of files arranged in folders.

I record them for study purposes, to improve my approach, my practice. But not just that.

I value the quiver in their voices. That fragility. That gentleness. I cherish their mangled, approximate, confused words, and their silences.

And I save all the recordings, even after they're dead.

I started making recordings of Mrs Seld in our fifth or sixth session. I've kept them all.

I go into her room. She looks tired. I can tell immediately she isn't in a very cooperative mood. But she sits up and furtively pats her hair into place. She tries to give me a smile. I'm always really struck by old ladies' coquettishness.

I take out my equipment and put it on her desk: pen, notebook, picture book.

'How are you, Michka?'

'I'm fine.'

'That's a "fine but not great" – am I right?'

'I'm having a bit of trouble adopting . . . adepting.'

'Adapting?'

'Yes, that's it.'

'That's understandable. It takes a few weeks to find your feet. You haven't been here that long. I've brought some things for us to work on together today. Is that OK?'

She looks at me distrustfully.

'What's that?'

'They're exercises specially designed for older people.'

'Why do you call them "older people"? You should say "the old". "The old" is fine. It's best to call a staid a staid. You'd say "the young", wouldn't you? You don't say "younger people".'

'You're right. Words matter to you, Michka; I like that. Would you like to do a little exercise?'

'Wouldn't you rather have a little cigarette?'

'Do you smoke?'

'No, no, not at all. I stopped . . . long ago, but honestly, in the circumstantials, a little cigarette wouldn't be too such.'

'It's forbidden throughout the building, Mrs Seld. And in any case, it wouldn't be very sensible. I don't smoke, anyway.'

She seems disappointed.

She sits quietly, watching me. Silence doesn't make her feel awkward. She studies every detail of my appearance: my watch, my socks, my hair.

'OK, right, Michka. I'll ask you a question, then show you four pictures and you have to pick the right answer. Then you have to try to give the right name for the object.'

She's listening carefully. I'm gesticulating as I speak.

'Try this one as an example. What tool is used to spread cement?'

I put four pictures in front of her – a trowel, a spade, secateurs and a rake – which she looks at with an air of mock puzzlement.

'This isn't a bungle of laughs.'

'It's not the funniest example, I grant you.'

'I'd rather just chat.'

'OK, we'll talk for a bit and then we can do some exercises.'

'There's a lady who comes into my room.'

'Here?'

'Yes, she's come several times in the evening. Comes in, just like that, with no warming and says she's looking for the little boy. She scares me.'

'Is she a resident?'

'Yes, but yesterday, something happened, you know. Yesterday she came in after dinner, the same time as before, and asked me where the little boy was and I . . . I said . . . all . . . no-nonsince, so that she understood, "I don't know where the little boy is, but I must warm you that you're making a mistake." I'd put the television on, even though I don't really watch it, but it's because there's . . . this presenter I like, who's got really bright teeth, rather neatly turned out, you know? The one who says the news. So imagine, when this woman heard his voice, the stake she got herself into! She suddenly started arguing with me and shouting, "But he's there, the little boy!" as though I'd stolen her little boy for my television. So I can tell you, I immediately switched it off with the . . . TV- . . . demote – boom! – so she'd go away. And it worked. But now I can't turn it on again. I'm scared she'll come back, you see . . .'

'You need to talk to the care assistants. They'll go and see the woman, who's maybe losing the plot a bit, and make sure she doesn't come back into your room uninvited.'

She doesn't say anything for a moment. And then she looks me in the eye.

'It's not going to work out, is it?'

'What isn't?'

'Everything. Everything that's stripping away, just like that, so quickly. It's not going to work out.'

'We're going to work together, if you're up for it, Michka, so that it does work out.'

'In . . . all honestly?'

I hesitate for a second before answering.

'We can slow things down, but we can't stop them.'

The furniture in the room in the nursing home has been rearranged so that the back wall is completely bare.

Michka's in the middle of the room, frozen in a strange posture, as though halted in her tracks.

A little girl's voice breaks the silence: 'One . . .'

Michka at once begins advancing towards the bare wall.

'Two . . . three . . . *Statues*!'

Michka suddenly stops mid-movement, in a position she has trouble maintaining. Then the little girl's voice again: 'One . . .'

She takes a few more steps forward.

'Two . . . three . . . *Statues*!'

Michka stops. This time she's in an awkward position. She sways and can't stay still.

The child's voice is delighted.

'You moved! You moved! Back to the start!'

Michka goes back. She drags her feet a bit. She leans against the other wall.

But the child's voice won't let her have a break.

'Ready! One . . . two . . . three . . . *Statues!*'

This time Michka hasn't moved.

'Where's my stick? I've reached the point where I can't tell if I need it. You know what I mean? I feel fine, you see, the words are there, like they used to be, I don't even need to hunt for them, pick or pamper them, they come by themselves, straightforward, no fuss, no need to coax them, capture them, caress them, no. Look closely, they're coming and going freely. It's lovely. I'm in a dream, I know. It's not a nightmare this time. Look closely, look at the colours, the shape of things; you can tell at once it isn't a nightmare. I'll need to talk to you about it. Yes, I'll tell you I had a dream and all the words were there, all of them. I didn't need your cards or your pictures or your lists. Everything was as simple as it used to be and it was so joyful, so nice, you know. It makes me so tired, always hunting, hunting, hunting. It's exhausting. It's draining. It's wearying. I don't need anything else, you know. Nothing at all. Mrs Danville brought me chocolates. She was the caretaker in our building when Marie was little, ages ago – have I told you about her? Mrs Danville's very nice and the chocolates are delicious. So you see, I don't need anything else. If the words come back, things will be fine, absolutely fine. And I won't give a fig about everything else. Even that woman who goes out in her car almost every day. Who does she think she is? Mocking us with her car. Almost every day. Yes, she's a resident, you know, she'll go for a spin round town, just like that, almost every day, with her little headscarf on. She thinks she's Grace Kelly or something, almost every day. But if that's the case, she could have stayed in her own home. Why has she come here if she's so independent? It gets on my nerves, I tell you. But I don't care, since the words are back, so there's no need to do the exercises any more. But you could still come and see me all the same. Just to chat from time to time. It would be a pity not to, because you're so handsome. I don't like men wearing earrings, but it looks good on you, especially when you put in the little black stud, the tiny little one. It's actually quite pretty.'

The little girl's voice resumes: 'One . . . two . . . three . . . *Statues*!'

Michka has rushed towards the other side of the room and, in one bound, touched the wall.

She smiles.

'This time it must be a dream! I'll tell you about it tomorrow. You'll enjoy it, a dream like this.'

I knock and go in.

I find her lying on her bed, which is unusual. She hates being surprised when she's dozing. She sits up at once and looks around for the book she'd put down by her side.

'Hello, Michka, how are you?'

'I'm fine . . .'

'Are you tired?'

'A little.'

'Has Marie been to see you?'

'Yes, she came yesterday. Do you know her?'

'You often tell me about her, but I haven't met her. She mainly comes at the weekend and I'm here in the week . . .'

'Ah yes, that's right. Yes, yes.'

'I'll give you a few minutes. I'll set up my equipment on your desk.'

'Oh . . . are you sure?'

'Yes, I'm sure. Don't you want to get up?'

'Yes, I do . . . but . . . it's those exercises, you know . . . they're such a snore.'

I help her get up from the bed and then give her my arm and walk her over to the chair. She walks slowly. I suspect she's taking her time to put off the moment of getting down to work.

'So, have you been able to watch television, Michka?'

'Not so much as such.'

'Why's that?'

'Well, you know, there's no point. They talk too quickly. Even the pictures often go too quickly. I used to like that man who . . . flies off, you know, all over, the young chap with the rugsack, who sleeps in people's houses all round the world . . . he's very funny. He bumps into people and sleeps in their homes in his sleepy bag, do you know him? I really liked him, but just at the moment I can't find him. What about you? Do you watch television?'

'Not a lot, Michka. There are programmes I like, but I don't have the time. I've got a lot of patients this year and I've also gone back to my studies.'

She suddenly looks very interested.

'Oh really, what are you studying?'

'It's a university degree, to continue my training.'

'In what neck of the wood?'

'Neuropsychological rehabilitation.'

'Ah . . . that's tough.'

'Yes, but fascinating.'

'But it's not working.'

'Yes, yes, it is. I'm coping.'

'No, not you. The . . . repair.'

'It is, Michka, you'll see. We can improve lots of things. Anyway, it's just the right moment. I've prepared a little exercise about travel. Are you up for it?'

She gives me a hangdog look.

Instead of sitting in the upright chair, she slumps into her armchair.

'Can you bring me my stick? You never know, I might be able to . . . gun for it . . . in an emergency.'

'Run for it? Why do you want to run for it?'

'If the alarm goes off. It happened the other day. Weren't you here? After lunch, we were down the stairs, almost all of us, apart from the fourth floor, but all of us resistants, we'd just had our little crème camarel when out of the blue the sirens started shrieking . . . It was so loud!'

'The alarm?'

'Yes, that's it! It gave me such a scart! That's why I like to have my stick to hand, just in case . . . What about you?'

I try to follow her train of thought, but she clarifies for me.

'How old are you?'

'Thirty-five.'

'Ah, good.'

For a few seconds, she seems to be processing this information and it occurs to me that she may be making a list of all the things you can do when you're thirty-five that are now beyond her.

'And you like old people.'

'Well, I suppose . . . I—I like working with old people, yes. I find it . . . interesting.'

'Really? That's strange . . . Truly. For all that we have left to say.'

'Well, exactly, I try to help you to say . . . all that you have to say. And often it's very interesting.'

'Ah yes, well, when you put it . . . that's good . . . What about your parents, are they old?'

'My mother died a few years back. Before she got old, to be honest.'

'Ah, that's good.'

'Well, that's one way of looking at it . . . There's probably an upside, but also quite a big downside. I'd have preferred to have her around a bit longer.'

'You had things left to say?'

I've already noticed this, old people's remarkable sharpness. The way they sometimes pinpoint the exact spot that hurts.

'Yes, Michka, I still had things to say. I hope I showed it, but I hadn't said everything.'

'Ah, that's alloying . . . annoying.'

'Yes. Right then, are we going to give this exercise a go?'

44

'Off course.'

'Do you remember the one we did last time?'

'Yes.'

'So this is virtually the same idea, except this time I'll give you several words and you have to find the common term that links them. For example: Buddhism, Protestantism, Catholicism . . . The word that links them is . . .'

'What about your father?'

I'd like to have a joker I could play when I wanted to, or else feign incomprehension, but Michka isn't one to let herself be hoodwinked.

'I don't see him.'

'Really? Why?'

'It would take too long to explain.'

'I've all the time.'

'But I've got work to do, Michka.'

'Is your father alive?'

'Yes.'

'Is he old?'

'I suppose so.'

'And you haven't seen him since he got old?'

'No.'

'I see.'

'What do you see?'

'Why you're so keen on the elderly.'

'Well, maybe . . . I've never thought of it like that.'

'Well, you need to tell him.'

'Tell him what?'

'Everything. Everything you reject . . . regret, after-wards, when people disappear – pff! – just like that. You see? It happens, you know. You can't keep carry-ing all that around inside. It'll give you nightcares . . . nightmares afterwards, you know.'

'Yes, yes, I know. We'll see, eh? . . . OK, let's continue. Four more words: bitter, acidic, salty, sweet . . .'

'Taste?'

'Very good. Here's another—'

'All the same, isn't it a pity . . .'

'What is?'

'Mrs Danville's fruit jellies. I haven't got a single one left . . .'

'I thought you preferred chocolates?'

'That's number-two choice. But fruit jellies are number one. Did your father upset you?'

I can't hold back a sigh.

'Yes, Michka.'

'Ah, that's diffu—. . . difficult.'

I don't know if she's talking about the exercise I'm trying to get her to do or my situation. She's looking at me as though she expects me to tell her the whole story immediately.

'You should go and see.'

'See what?'

'How he is. Your father.'

'He's fine, as far as I know.'

'Was it a long time ago?'

'Yes, a very long time ago.'

'That's too bad. You need to know, all the same. If you can pick up again, you can repair things.'

'No, Michka, it can't be repaired.'

'So, it's serious?'

'It's painful.'

'Ah . . . but . . . you should maybe . . .'

She's watching me. I can't tell what she's thinking.

'Right, Michka, let's get down to it. Listen carefully: antique dealer, record dealer, bookseller, cabinet maker . . . What's the term that links them all?'

'Disappeared?'

MARIE

For a few weeks, she's just been sitting in her room, not reading or watching television. Dozing.

I knock on her door and wait for her to tell me to come in.

'Is that you?'

'Yes, Michk', it's me. How are you?'

'Oh, not so bad . . . I didn't know you were coming. I had it down for tomorrow, but I don't know why, I wasn't too . . . compedent.'

'You weren't confident? That's understandable, I said Friday or Saturday. You're not too tired?'

'No, I'm fine. That's not the problem.'

'So what *is* the problem?'

'These words that elide me . . .' (There's a long pause.) 'Collude me . . .' (She sighs.) 'You see?'

'I know, Michka. But all the same, you've still got plenty in stock, and you also invent new ones. Has the speech therapist been to see you?'

'Yes, yes. But it's . . . it's not . . . The exercises are diffu— . . . are diffi— . . . difficult. Do you want to see?'

She hands me a piece of paper with words and drawings on.

'Do you have to guess the opposites?'

'No, the cinnamons.'

'Synonyms?'

'Exactly. But I've had enough of syno— . . . those things. You know, the right word alludes me. And anyway, it's pointless, I know full well how this will end. Eventually there'll be nothing left to fill the blank, no words, you know, or just some old nonsense. Can you imagine, an old biddy, all alone, drizzling on . . . frizzling on . . .'

'We're not there yet.'

'We're not far off, believe me. The end isn't that far, Marie, you know. I mean the end when the head's gone, kaput, pff, and all the words too. You can't know when the body will pack up, of course, but the head's already started. The words pack their bags and off they go.'

'No, no, Michka. Are you going to the memory workshop?'

'I'm not keen. I prefer it when that lad comes . . . He's very handsome, you know. You should meet him.'

'But it needn't be either/or, Michk'. The speech therapist comes to you twice a week, but you can go down to the memory workshop on Wednesdays with the others. Have you tried it yet?'

'Not keen. There's one woman who answers everything, just like that, straight off . . . not a moment's hesitation. Point blank, she comes out with the right answer. She knows every actual and imaginal word. She acts all proud, you know, and that gets under my shin. Why does she come if she already knows it all? Also, she could get dressed, but no, oh no, she spends her life in her dressing down as though that was the height of fashion . . .'

'Maybe she feels more comfortable like that.'

'Yes, well, a little bit of recency never hurt anyone. Why are you laughing? Oh well, you can laugh . . . But you know, you've got better things to do. Truly. You shouldn't come so often. You'll get sick of it.'

'Hey, Michka, we've already talked about this. I come because I enjoy coming.'

'You're wasting your time. And into the bargain, seeing me in this grate . . . in this fate . . . in this state . . . is pointless.'

'Listen, you came to see me when I was in hospital, didn't you? Do you remember?'

'Yes, I remember. When you were ill. You were so . . . it was like . . .'

For a moment, she's lost in thought.

'You know you almost died?'

'I know, Michk'. So when I spent days and days in that little room, you came to see me quite often, didn't you?'

She nods.

'So can I come to see you when I want?'

She gives me a smile.

'You don't tell me about how you are . . . how are things with you?'

'Fine. Everything's fine.'

'Work?'

'Fine. It's going OK. I'm starting to look after cases on my own. It's very interesting.'

'It's not too far for you to travel?'

'No, it's fine on the train. In fact, it's quick.'

'Are you looking after yourself?'

'Yes, don't worry.'

She looks at me for a moment.

'Have you done your hair?'

'Yes, Michk', I've done my hair.'

'You look a bit . . . peely. Are you eating properly?'

'Yes, fine.'

'You know, we've got a new resistant at our table in the canteen. Did I tell you?'

'A new resident?'

'Yes, she never stops talking, so I pretend to be death in one ear and that way I don't have to answer her. Never stops, you can't imagine, a continulous flow. Talk, talk. It doesn't bother her in the slightest, as though she was the only person in the world. So me and Armande – you know Armande, the woman I like – we do this . . .'

For a few seconds, she pretends to be absorbed in eating and unable to hear anyone talking to her.

'Does it work?'

'These are old ladies' stories. Marie, you should say to me, "Careful, Michka, you're telling old ladies' stories." I don't want you to think I'm grouting . . . I'm grousing, but it does me good to sound off. I don't have it so bad, you know, the people are really nice, but I liked it better at home.'

'I know, Michka, but you couldn't stay at home any more, do you remember?'

'Yes, I remember.'

She goes quiet for a moment and looks thoughtful. Then she leans forward. She speaks softly, like she's sharing a secret.

'You know, Marie, I wanted to ask you something that I can't do. I want to put a . . . card . . . in the paper.'

'A card?'

'Yes, you know, like we did before. In the paper, to look for people.'

'An ad?'

'Yes.'

'You mean the ad we put in *Le Monde*?'

'Yes.'

'You want to have another go at finding the people who took you in when you were little?'

'Yes.'

I look at her for a moment, taking stock of what this means to her. What it means now. I notice a tiny tremor in her chin, a sign of distress or emotion that's appeared since she came here, which she's probably unaware of.

'OK, Michka, of course. I'll take care of it. But you mustn't get your hopes up, OK? You know we've already tried. The problem is we don't know their name.'

'Yes, I know.'

'I'll put in the same ad and I'll give my details just in case, all right?'

'Yes, all night. Thank you. Thank you very much. And let know how much it costs.'

'Don't worry about that. We'll give it a go, but you know there's not much chance it'll work.'

'I know.'

'Shall we go into the garden for a bit?'

'Yes, that would be nice. I'll put on the . . . piece . . . the fleece you gave me. Grace Kelly never takes her spies off it. She'd love one just like it, I tell you.'

The nasty director bursts into Michka's room. She hasn't knocked and regards a greeting as unnecessary. She's furiously brandishing a copy of *Le Monde*.

'Did you put this ad in?'

Michka nods. The director explodes.

'This cannot be happening! Who do you think you are, Mrs Seld? You are completely mad! Completely out of your mind! Utterly thoughtless! An ad? Why not a poster campaign while you're at it? A TV campaign? A hot-air balloon? A plane trailing a banner at the beach? It's almost beyond belief . . . an ad! We are in the twenty-first century, Mrs Seld. The war is over. Our business is growing, expanding, booming, and you take it upon yourself to insert this ad, which could damage our reputation? Do you know what reputation is? Do you have the slightest idea what it represents? These days it means money! It can sink you in less than twenty-four hours!'

Michka says nothing. She remains sitting on her bed like a little girl, her hands on her thighs.

The director opens the paper at the small ads. She reads aloud, making no attempt to conceal her irony: '"Michèle Seld, known as Michka, seeks Nicole and Henri, who took care of her from 1942 to 1945 at La Ferté-sous-Jouarre." Nicole and Henri! Don't you even know their surname?'

'No.'

'These are the people who saved you and you don't even remember their name? And you don't even go to the memory workshop! It's shameful . . . And are you sure about their first names? And the village, are you sure about that?'

Michka is paralysed, dumbstruck.

'And none of this robs you of your appetite! Mrs Danville's chocolates are fine! A little apple juice, that's fine! Celeriac salad – fine! But when it comes to doing Mr Milloux's exercises, it's a complete no-show . . . That's a disaster, a washout! You have a private room, you eat well, you go to the cinema club, you enjoy the garden. You don't need me to tell you that you cost our establishment a lot of money, Mrs Seld, a *lot* of money! But what do you give us in return? Mmm? It does pose serious profitability issues, you must admit, and it cannot go on, I'm sorry to have to tell you, because you contribute nothing. I'm choosing my words carefully:

nothing. What are you thinking of? They're dead! Dead! Dead! Dead! The truth is they are dead, and you never thanked them!'

Michka wakes up in a sweat, sitting up in bed.

Her heart's pounding, she's struggling to get her breath back. She hides her head in her hands and stifles a sob.

A few days later when I come into her room, I find her standing in the middle of the floor, trembling, leaning on her stick.

'I do know how to make my bed. It takes me time, lots of time, I'm not defying it, but I know. And every day she does it again behind my back. She starts again, every morning, she pulls on the . . . breadspread, you see, as if I've done it wrong.'

'Who do you mean?'

'The care assistant.'

'You need to tell her, Michka, that you don't want her going behind your back.'

'I told her! But she droles her eyes, like I'm a stupid old biddy.'

'She's probably just trying to help. Do you want me to talk to her?'

'No, no, you have other things to say. But it's the same with the shower. The new commandant doesn't want me to go in on my own.'

'I know, Michka, but that's because you fell the other day, so that's understandable. It's for your own good, to stop you hurting yourself.'

'Yes, but my . . . my good isn't that, Marie. My good is to be . . .'

For a few seconds she hunts for words that she can't find.

'Left in peace?'

'Yes, exactly. Left in peace. All the time there's some-one coming in here. Bringing breadfast, or pills, giving me laundry, making the bed, the homework, asking how I am, warming me about this or that, all the time, all the time, knock, knock, and in they come. Can you imagine? And if you don't want to see them, you can't . . . disappear.'

'I know that, Michk'. I understand. Don't you want to sit down for a bit?'

She slumps into her chair.

'So did you put the card in?'

'Yes, Michka, it'll be in *Le Monde* this week, and next week it'll go in *Le Figaro*. I'll tell you if I hear anything.'

She takes this information on board.

From now on, she will wait. Hope. She won't dare ask me about it, but for as long as she can, she'll keep this window half-open on hope.

'It's the same thing with my wool-overs, you know. I do know how to put them away myself. Why's she sticking her nose in?'

'Hang on, shouldn't you be worrying about her finding your bottle of whisky instead?'

'It's well hidden, believe me. Better than ever. But I don't like being frisked. But what about you? What have you got to tell me?'

'Everything's fine, Michka.'

She looks at me for a moment.

'Have you done your hair?'

'Yes, I've done my hair, Michk'. As I've said, curly hair like mine is hard work. You can't do your hair like everyone else . . .'

'I see . . . if you say so. That's a pity.'

There's a short silence. We're both thinking.

'Actually, I do have something to tell you, Michka . . . I'm expecting a baby.'

She pretends she didn't hear.

'I've got chocolates, if you want one, with a drop of alcohol, not much. Barely any. They're scrumptious. It was Mrs Danville who brought them.'

'Michk', did you hear what I said?'

'Which boy was it?'

'What do you mean, which boy?'

She's suddenly outraged.

'Don't you know which boy it was?'

'Yes, of course I know, but I don't think he wants to have a child.'

'Is he a new one?'

'Yes. Well, no, not that new. I suppose it's been a few months. He's called Lucas. I've mentioned him a couple of times. I met him at a party. He's very nice, but we don't live together, plus . . . he has to go abroad. You know, I didn't think I could get pregnant. The doctor at the hospital, you remember, told me there would probably be lasting damage, that it could be complicated. That's why.'

'That's true . . . when you were ill, you were so . . .'

She makes an odd gesture, miming something vanishing into the air.

'You were all . . . It's true. So it's amazing you're inspecting.'

'Yes, that's it exactly, I'm expecting, Michk', and I'm really scared.'

I watch for her reaction for a moment, looking for encouragement or disapproval. But she looks at me in silence, more attentive than ever.

'Have you told the boy?'

'No, not yet. I wanted to have things straight in my own head first. You know, Michk', I'm scared . . . I don't know if I'm up to it, having a child. I'm scared I won't cope. I'm scared of passing things on or them being passed on in spite of me, like a curse, or fate. Something that'll be there in the shadows, in memories, in the blood, like part of the historical record, something inevitable. Do you know what I mean? And do I have enough love? Am I caring and patient enough? How can I know if I'm capable of bringing up a child, of hugging them, taking care of them? Will I be able to talk to them, tell them the stuff that matters, let them climb on a big toboggan, cross the road alone, give them my hand when they need it? Will I know what to do? I'm scared I won't love them and I'm scared of loving them too much. I'm scared of hurting them and scared they won't love me.'

'What a shame . . . When I've finished Mrs Danville's new chocolates, what will I be able to offer visitors?'

'Maybe it'd be better to have an abortion.'

'Oh no, not that.'

'What do you mean, "oh no"?'

'No, no, no . . . And it's got nothing to do with that woman, she always looks good with her impeccable chignon, dressed up to the mines.'

She sees my stunned expression.

'Oh, you know who I mean, that woman who got out of the camps . . .'

'Simone Veil?'

'That's it. It's really very good, what she did for women. Terrificent, even. But it's got nothing to do with her.'

'No. Quite . . .'

She returns to her thoughts, visibly moved. I break the silence.

'Are you managing to read?'

'It's so small.'

'But I brought you those large-print books. Did you try them?'

'Which ones?'

'The books I brought last time. With large print.'

'Large print? Those are for old people . . . I lent them to that chap.'

'Which chap?'

'That chap. He showed me how to open my window. The whole way. It's not allowed. With a fife.'

'Who is he? Does he work here?'

'No, no. It's not allowed, as I said.'

'Who is he then?'

'The chap next door. I can't make it plainer. You've seen him before. He's got a tweet suit.'

'Mr Terdian?'

'Yes. I can tell he knows his way around this place, the length of time he's been here. He showed me, with a . . . a . . .' (she sighs) ' . . . a . . . crack! In fact, you can get the window to open wide, but you're not supposed to. So when they come, hup!' (She mimes jumping up to the window, while staying where she is.) 'I shut it.'

'Just be careful you don't take a tumble!'

'You need a really sharp one. I took one from the dining room the night we had rose . . . beef . . .'

'Roast beef?'

'You know, I didn't have any . . .'

'Roast beef?'

'Children.'

'I know, Michk'. But you've got me. I'm here.'

'You cried a lot, you know. When that doctor told you, when he said it wasn't certain, not at all certain, that you'd ever be inspecting. You cried a lot, I can tell you.'

'That's true. But maybe now isn't the right time.'

She looks out the window and then turns back to me.

'You know, I didn't want children. Not one bit. No family and no children. Absolutely nothing. If you hadn't lived upstairs, I'd have stayed like that. I was just a labour . . . a neighbour, living by my shelf. When you came that first time, do you remember, because you'd been home alone – how long? A day or two? – you didn't want to say, well, I was scared then too. You had some-thing to eat and went back upstairs alone. I didn't sleep a blink all night. And then you came back a second time, with those eyes, those big eyes that made me feel worse, so I took you in. And then next, every time, you'd come back and I'd take you in, whole afternoons, and then I bought felt tips and coloured paper and scissors, and then zoo maminals – do you remember? – little plastic zebras – you liked them best – then modelling clay, and then Mr Strawberry; we put them in the . . . frozer. You came back every evening just about. That's exactly how it happened: a little girl ringing my doorbell. You stayed over when things went bear-shaped, when it all went wrong, and then after, there was, well. That's not the most important thing, I mustn't get things mixed up . . . sorry. You're the one who must decide. You're the one who'll know. But I just want to say one thing and then you'll take your solution: that's what counts, more than anything.'

'What does?'

'For the first time in my strife, I began to take care of someone else, someone other than myself, I mean. That's what changes everything, you know, Marie. It's being afraid for someone else, not just yourself. It's a great opportunity you have.'

'You see, you do have the words.'

She's flattered.

'Ah yes, it's true . . . in a mergency.'

'Would you like me to fetch you tea from the machine?'

'That'd be nice. I'm exhausted, you know. With melon, please.'

'Lemon?'

'That's it.'

Michka gets dressed up the days she's expecting a visitor. She selects her pale blue pullover, which brings out the colour of her eyes, or puts on her beige jacket, which matches her trousers.

I always call her before I visit. Ideally the day before, so that she has time to prepare.

I knock before going in and greet her with a kiss.

'You shouldn't come. You'll get bored. Plus, you should be resting.'

'We've already been through this, Michk'. I come because I enjoy it. How are you feeling?'

'I'm fine . . . but I'm not sure what's going on.'

'What do you mean?'

'Here. It's not at all like it used to be. The standard's going down, you know. Two of the presidents have died . . .'

'Residents?'

'Yes. Two in one week. Mrs Crespin, who got those parcels with the salamis in, well . . . in the night, pff, just like that.'

'That must have been upsetting . . . You were fond of Mrs Crespin.'

'Yes . . . But, you know, we're old ladies. I've already told you, you have to be . . . realistical. There comes a time when it can't go on. It's even for the best. It's not sad, but it is scary.'

'And did you know the other person?'

'No, she was on the fourth . . . The fourth floor. With the . . . They're not crazy, you know, but they're like ghosts that roam at night, so they have to be shut up. But the problemo's about the catalogue . . .'

'Which catalogue?'

'You know, the catalogue for the Trois Ssss . . .' (she hesitates) ' . . . Suisses.'

'Why?'

'It was hers.'

'Mrs Crespin's?'

'Yes, she lent it to me so that I could get some songs . . . socks, and I'm embarrassed because I didn't give it back to her.'

'It's not that important, Michka, I doubt she'd've been able to take it with her. Did you see any you liked?'

'No, I don't like pompoms . . . But you know, it's not like it used to be here. Especially in the evenings, when they do the rounds.'

'What rounds, Michk'?'

'When all the presidents are in their rooms, they go round giving out the . . . and also in the mornings. I know what that means.'

'You're fretting over nothing. I told you, it's perfectly normal for the care assistants to do a little tour to see that everything's OK.'

'I don't like the nights.'

'Aren't you sleeping well?'

'I told you, it's because of the words . . . It's at night that they go to ground . . . they get lost, when I can't sleep, I know that's when they varnish . . . misappear. I'm certain. But there's nothing I can do. Whole truckloads, at top speed. There's nothing to be done about it, I can tell you. Even the speech thep . . . thepar . . . therat . . .'

'Therapist?'

'Yes, he told me. The exercises don't help any more when you get to my stage.'

'You're exaggerating. I'm sure he didn't say that. It's because you don't like those exercises.'

'It's exhausting. You should see me after – good for nothing. It's sad, you know . . .'

She remains lost in thought for a moment.

'People shouldn't get old. But it's good you're here. I wanted to tell you I've had a think and I'd prefer a cremotion.'

'You what?'

'For my funereal. A cremotion . . . a few little sand-wiches and that's it. Like Mrs Crespin. Apparently hers was lovely.'

68

'Do you mean a cremation?'

'That's right, but spammon sandwiches, not pâté.'

'Salmon? OK, right, got it. But there's no urgency, you know. We're not in a rush.'

'I couldn't go to Mrs Crespin's. They'd laid on a wagon to take us all together, but I was too tired.'

'I understand, Michk'. That's understandable. You need your rest.'

'And the little one?'

'Which little one?'

(I knew what she meant.)

'*Your* little one! Where is he?'

'Well, he's still there. I've talked to Lucas. He's been very understanding, but he's decided to go to India. He works for Nouvelles Frontières, the travel company, and they've offered him a job as local rep. He knows the country well. He told me at the start he was waiting for this job. And I said at the start I didn't want to move.'

'Why?'

'Well . . . because you're here, Michk', and in any case, I've got no reason to go and live in India. I've just found the kind of job I was looking for, so it's already complicated enough . . .'

'And the boy – is he hungry . . . hangry?'

'Angry? No. He said I could keep the baby if I wanted to. That he'd help me when he could. But he wants to go. Whatever happens. And he's not especially keen to have a child. You know, I don't think he's all that in love with me.'

'Really? Why?'

(If I'd told her he'd turned down a cheque for five million euros, she'd have reacted with the same surprise.)

'Well, that's life, Michk'. It's just how it is.'

'But did you explain why you couldn't do your hair, because of how it is?'

'Don't worry, Michk', it's got nothing to do with my hair . . . he's got dreadlocks. Do you know what they are?'

'Yes, yes. Oh well. You'll have to make your solution all alone then. Without a fiancé.'

'Yes, that's right. But it'll be OK. I'll manage . . . Anyway, I think I really want a baby. Do you fancy a walk outside?'

'No, not today. I'm tired.'

'Are you sure? It's a nice day.'

'No tanks.'

JÉRÔME

She's in her armchair, waiting for me.

She's not doing anything as she waits. She's not pretending to read or knit or be busy.

Waiting's a full-time job here.

When I go into her room, I shake her hand and ask for her news. She offers me a glass of water, or fruit juice if she has a little carton left over from teatime. She likes to be able to give me a chocolate or a sweet as a way of doing something for me, I know.

We have our rituals.

She likes the moment when I press 'Record' on my digital recorder and our session begins, always with more or less the same formula: 'It's the fifth of September and I'm recording my twentieth session with Mrs Seld, with her consent.'

'Do you like proverbs, Michka?'

She makes a face.

'Today we're going to do a little exercise to stimulate your memory and help you maintain your vocabulary.'

'We'll see.'

'Yes, we'll see. It's a lot of fun. I'll give you the start of a proverb, and you have to think how it ends. We'll begin with something easy. You just have to guess the last words to complete the saying. OK?'

She nods unenthusiastically.

'"Sufficient unto each day the . . ."'

'Easel.'

'Are you sure? I'll say it again: "Sufficient unto each day the . . ."'

'Weevil.'

'"The *evil* thereof", Michka. You almost got it. "He who is absent is always in the . . ."'

'Strong . . . wrong!'

'Very good! "There's no smoke without . . ."'

'Fire.'

'"Truth lies at the bottom of a . . ."'

'Field? . . .' (She ponders.) 'Volcano?'

She's now looking at me with a vexed expression.

'I don't know that one.'

'"Truth lies at the bottom of a well." That one doesn't ring a bell?'

'Not at all.'

'Here's another: "A fault confessed is half . . ."?'

'Hmm. So, have you been?'

'Where?'

'To see your father.'

'I didn't say I'd go, Michka. I said I'd think about it.'

'Have you thought about it?'

'Yes, I'm thinking, but it takes time. You can't decide just like that. It's risky. And complicated. So don't use that as an excuse to stop concentrating. Here's another: "To have other fish to . . ."'

'It makes me afraid for you. The regrets.'

'I know, Michka. It makes me afraid too. But sometimes there's no choice. It's a matter of . . . protecting yourself.'

'But you're strong now, aren't you?'

The nurse comes into her room at just the right moment. I leave my recorder running.

He enunciates very loudly, as though speaking to a child. Michka doesn't seem to take offence.

'Did you want to see me, Mrs Seld? I heard you were looking for me this morning . . .'

'Ah yes . . . Do you think you could give me something more . . . substantial in my . . . in the evening . . . the cap . . . cu . . .'

'In your teacup?'

'No, no . . . The tiny little things, like that. You put them here and there . . . two or three . . .'

'Capsules?'

73

'Yes.'

'You mean your treatment, Mrs Seld. You have a pill that you take at six p.m. And then a bit later you get another.'

'What are they called?'

'At six it's Omeprazole and at ten it's Mianserin.'

'Which is more charmful?'

'They do different things. The one at ten o'clock is to give you a good night's sleep and the one at six is to stop you getting stomach ache . . .'

'Ah, so give me a ten o'clock.'

'I'd have to ask your doctor about that. Do you want to have the ten o'clock brought forward?'

'Yes.'

'You're not managing to get to sleep, is that it?'

'That's a bit strong, but not much.'

'We'll ask your doctor. Apparently you're distressed in the evening.'

'Oh, not so much as such.'

Then he turns to me, as a witness.

'You realise that her and Mr Terdian were keeping knives in their rooms to tamper with the windows . . .'

Then he speaks to her again, much more loudly.

'We can't let you have knives in your room, Mrs Seld, do you understand?'

She adopts a slightly haughty tone.

'Yes, I've fully understood. But that's no big squeal. We can open the window – we won't misappear!'

'I'll speak to the director about your medication and she'll raise it with your doctor. I'll be off now, Mrs Seld.'

As he goes, his shoes sound like suction cups on the lino.

Michka looks at me.

'He's nice, you know. He may seem a bit of a witnit, but he's very nice.'

'I don't doubt it, Michka. Shall we get back to our exercise?'

Her shoulders slump and she sighs melodramatically.

I laugh.

She laughs too.

'"He who can do the most can do . . ."'

'Did I tell you Marie's inspecting?'

'Expecting? Yes, you told me last week.'

'She's going to keep the baby. On her own, you know.'

'Are you worried about that?'

'Not so much as such. But a bit all the same.'

MARIE

When I go to visit Michka, I observe the other residents. The very, very old ladies, the ones in the middle and the not-so-old, and sometimes I want to ask them: does anyone caress you any more? Does anyone take you in their arms? How long is it since someone else's skin touched yours?

When I imagine being old, really old, when I try to project myself forty or fifty years into the future, the most painful, the most unbearable thing that strikes me is the thought that no one will touch me any more. The gradual, or sudden, disappearance of physical contact.

Perhaps their need is less, maybe the body withdraws, dries up, hardens like during a long fast. Or perhaps, on the contrary, it cries with longing, a silent, unbearable cry that no one hears.

When Michk' comes tottering towards me, precariously balanced, I'd like to hold her tight, breathe some of my energy, my strength into her.

But I stop short of taking her in my arms. Awkwardness, probably. And the fear of hurting her.

She's become so frail.

When I'm old, I'll stretch out on my bed or settle back in an armchair and listen to the same music I listen to now, the stuff they play on the radio or in nightclubs. I'll close my eyes to re-experience the feeling of my body dancing. My body relaxed, supple, obedient, my body among other bodies, my body free of anyone watching, when I dance alone in the middle of the living room. When I'm old, I'll spend hours like that, attentive to every sound, every note, every impulse. Yes, I shall close my eyes and project my mind back into the dance, the trance, I'll recover one by one the movements, the breaks, and my body will again meld with the rhythm, the beat, in perfect time with its pulse.

When I'm old, if I make it that far, I'll still have that. The memory of the dance, the bass pounding in my stomach, and the sway of my hips.

She's dozing in her armchair. I've been sitting beside her for a few minutes. Tiny ripples pass across her face and I can tell she's becoming aware of my presence. She opens her eyes.

'Hello, Michk', how are you?'

'I wasn't asleep, you know.'

'I know, Michk', don't worry. You were waiting for me. Are you feeling OK?'

'Yes, fine. And what about you? How are things with the . . . little one?'

'I saw the doctor. He said everything was fine.'

'That's good. And the card?'

'Still nothing, Michk', I'm sorry. I put the ad in again on Tuesday. But no word so far.'

Her face seems suddenly to droop with sadness.

'I so wished . . . you know . . .'

'Have you really decided?'

'Yes.'

'I'll have a think, then. We'll try another way.'

She remains silent for a moment, lost in thought. And then she banishes her disappointment, like an unwelcome thought.

'They've suggested I play fridge, did I tell you?'

'No, you didn't. Who's "they"?'

'Those women.'

'Which women?'

'The young ones who're always hanging around downstairs, all afternoon, in the big room. Some of them even go to the body workshop.'

'It's true they look in good shape, but they're not that young, you know.'

'The one in the wheelchair is the leader of the pack. You know the one? With the dressing down.'

'Yes, I know. So did you say yes? Are you going to play bridge with them?'

'I don't know.'

'Why not? Don't you fancy it?'

'I'm scared I'll be out of step.'

'No, Michk'. You know the rules. There's no reason why you can't do it.'

'Oh, it's such a shame . . .'

'What is?'

'Mr Terdian had a fall in his room. He broke a big bone. He's down in the . . . in . . .' (She's searching for a word but can't find it.)

'In the infirmary?'

'Yes. I hope he'll come back.'

'Of course he will, Michk'. He'll be back when he feels better.'

'You know, all the same, there's something serious going on here. Very serious. In the toilets down the stairs. You need to go and see. I'm not setting foot in there any more, because I'm well aware of what they're up to.'

'What are you talking about, Michk'? Do you mean the toilets on the ground floor?'

'Yes, near the refec— . . . the refectuary . . . if you look above the door, there's a sort of . . . white thing . . . That sprays a . . . Pff, like that, every time you go in. I'm telling you: they're gassing us.'

'No, no, Michk', it's a room fragrancer.'

'The air's not sweet, believe me. And a bit of perfume won't make it sweeter. Take a look on your way out.'

'I will if you want me to. But don't fret over it. You're safe here. You know that.'

'If you say so.'

Michka stands opposite the nasty director.

The woman's expression and her stiff posture suggest that this is a nightmare, but at this moment, Michka isn't sure.

The director is speaking firmly, with a touch of impatience.

'Can you raise your arms, Mrs Seld?'

Michka obeys.

'Higher!'

Michka raises both arms to the sky.

'You've lost a great deal of suppleness since you arrived, Mrs Seld. A very great deal. It's common, I may as well tell you, this dramatic decline when residents enter an institution, but don't think we're going to feel sorry for you. We don't have time. The waiting list is long, you know. So, in summary: loss of independence in toileting, dressing . . .'

'Oh no, I get dressed by myself.'

'Not for much longer. If I may continue: loss of independence in toileting, dressing, eating . . .'

'No, I'm sorry, I have no problem feeding myself!'

'Increasingly incoherent language: aphasia, paraphasia, omitted words. A full house.'

'You know, in my dreams the words aren't missing. In my dreams I speak very clearly.'

'That's what you think. Or rather, that's what you would have us believe. But where's the proof?'

'Well, for example . . . I'm talking now, aren't I?'

The director starts laughing. A demonic laugh. Which suddenly stops.

'We're not debating it all night. Next question: what's your schedule?'

Michka looks troubled.

'I don't know . . .'

'Are you planning to linger in our establishment?'

'Not for too long, but I'm waiting for news. I can't just go off, you understand.'

'Well, you will have to make a big effort. One: make your bed properly, not like a teenager. Two: take part in the exercises that Mr Milloux suggests, which you obstinately refuse to join in with . . .'

'Not at all, I'm making a big effort.'

'Not enough. Three: respect the curfew. Four: remove your bottle of whisky from your cupboard.'

'Oh . . . you knew?'

'I know everything, Mrs Seld. The effective management of an old-age care facility is based on an impeccable intelligence service. What's your defence?'

'I'm sorry. I didn't mean to make you angry. Not at all. But you have to hide the little things, you see. To stay alive. We need to be able to do these little things in our own small corner, the little things that are slightly out of bounds, and close our door when we need some peace. Do you understand? It's not against you, Mrs . . .'

'Roastbeef.'

'It's not against you, Mrs Roastbeef. We just need to feel we still have a bit of freedom. Otherwise, what's the point?'

'Yes indeed, Mrs Seld! That's the real question: what is the point?'

With that, the director goes off, her footsteps echoing down the corridor.

JÉRÔME

Within a few weeks, her speech has become slower, more contorted. She sometimes stops mid-sentence, utterly lost, or else gives up on a missing word and goes straight to the next. I'm learning to follow her train of thought.

I'm beaten, I know. I recognise this tipping point. I don't know what causes it, but I see its effects. The battle's lost.

But I can't give up. Definitely not. Otherwise it will be even worse. Freefall.

We need to fight. Word by word. Step by step. Yield nothing. Not a single syllable or consonant. Without language, what's left?

We've done ten minutes of exercises, which she's graciously gone along with, but now it seems as though she's reached saturation point.

'Do you want to stop, Michka?'

'It's no point.'

'There is, I promise. There is a point.'

For a moment, she says nothing. Now that I know her, I realise these silences often come before a reminiscence or a confidence.

'What a shame. You know . . . I think about it so much . . . at night. Because of the card, in the paper. But no answer. I think about them. Imagine, three years . . . saying nothing . . . if ever . . . it was very dangerous, you know . . . they could have been . . . transported . . . them too . . . very dangerous . . . there was . . . a little . . . riverlet where we went . . . into the water . . . I

remember that . . . with the dog . . . I still have some . . .
like that . . . some . . . so clear . . . I would have loved
. . . so much . . . to be able to say. What a shame . . .'

'I'm sorry, Michka. I'm not following you too well.
Are you talking about your parents?'

'No, my parents . . . went . . . up in smoke.'

'You mean they were cremated?'

'Worse.'

I look at her for a moment. Her chin's begun to
tremble.

'Did you know them?'

'Not so much as such.'

'What year were you born, Michka?'

'Nineteen thirty-five.'

'Were your parents deported?'

She nods. Her face registers the brutal onslaught of
grief. She has no more words within her reach.

'Did they come back?'

She shakes her head.

She gets up and goes towards the bathroom.

She hasn't taken her stick. She knows this room by
heart. Every support. Right hand, left hand.

I say nothing. I wait.

I hear the sound of running water.

A few minutes later, she reappears and sits back
down. She gives me a smile.

'She comes less often, you know. With her being
inspecting.'

'Marie?'

'Yes. The doctor said that . . . not too much running aground.'

'She's probably got contractions. It's important not to take risks with the baby. Luckily Mrs Danville comes to see you from time to time.'

'Yes, and Armande. I'm fond of her. In the canteen, we're . . . slide by slide.'

'Ah yes, that lady looks very dynamic.'

'She does all the captivities, but I . . . I'm . . . too . . .'

'You're right, she takes part in lots of activities. But Michka, you're going to be a kind of grandmother!'

'Yes, so it seems. You know, it's odd . . . How to put it . . . there's a . . . a . . . sort of . . . ring, no? Or a . . . a . . .' (She makes a gesture like a circle or something complete.) 'Which takes shape . . . pit by pit . . . you see?'

'Tell me a bit more.'

'They're . . . pieces, that get put in place one by one, that look like . . . a j— . . . j— . . . j— . . .'

'Jigsaw?'

'That's it. That's the meaning. At the right moment. When you have trouble finding it . . . because everything's got so diffuse. You understand?'

'I think so.'

'And you haven't net Marie yet?'

'Met her?'

'That's it.'

'No, I haven't met her. She doesn't often come during the week and, as I told you, I'm never here at the weekend.'

'You know she lived . . . in the same block when she was . . . little?'

'Yes, Michka, you told me a lot about that soon after you came here.'

'I told you?'

'Yes, in our first sessions. You told me about Marie and you explained that she was the little girl who lived in the apartment upstairs, a little girl you often took care of. And there was also Mrs Danville, the caretaker of the block. She comes to see you regularly.'

'Yes, with the chocolates. She is so . . . nice. You know she . . . tel— . . . every day. Every morning. Brain or shine. Every morning before she starts her day.'

'She phones you?'

'Yes, that's right. It was the same when I still lived at home. Every day a quick rink to check up. Just think.'

'Yes, that's very nice, it's true. Is she still in the building?'

'No, she retired and went . . . out into the . . . greenery. You know, Marie went to her too when I couldn't look after her. But she mainly came to me.'

'What about Marie's parents?'

'The father – no one knows. And the mother, she was . . . such a sad young woman . . . Sometimes she spent the whole day shut up . . . without leaving her bed . . . sleeping, sleeping, all the time, you know, sheets closed, doors closed, eyes closed, but sometimes she'd take off just like that, without warming. First at night and then later, for days at the trot.'

'She left home?'

'That's right.'

I sense how affected she is by these memories. She rarely opens up about the past.

'I'd see her in the background, the little one . . . With her mother or by her shelf . . . Her . . . with dolls or . . . plastic stuff. One day I was out in the park . . . It was really cold. She was with her mother and they were having a . . .'

'Walk?'

'Yes, but the little one had no goat.'

'No coat?'

'Yes, she didn't have one. And her mother was talking and talking. She was kind to her but it was as if . . . she didn't realise. How cold it was. So I gave Marie my jumper and said: you can come and see me whenever you like.'

'Did she recognise you?'

'Yes, definitely. I often saw her in the . . . scarewell.'

'And did she come?'

'Yes, a few days later she knocked. I was . . . so . . . But what could I do? She had some dinner and then went home. But she came back . . . many times . . . She slept over too. And later she was with me nearly all the time.'

'Didn't you contact social services?'

'No, I thought about it, but I also thought about that word, you know . . . the word . . . that scares people.'

'What word, Michka?'

'The one that . . . tells on . . . A ver— . . . a ver— . . . a verb.'

'Inform?'

'Yes, inform. That was undrinkable. I didn't have the heart to . . . Her mother was trying to . . . get out . . . she was so . . . you know? She came to sleep at my place sometimes too. Some days she was absolutely fine, sometimes for quite a while. And then she'd look after the little one.'

'And now?'

'She's dead . . . Marie had just come of sage.'

'Of age?'

'That's right. There was an . . .' (She hunts for a word but can't find it.) 'In the car.'

'An accident?'

'Yes.'

'And then you looked after her?'

Silence enfolds us.

'All this brings back painful memories for you, doesn't it, Michka?'

'Yes, but now it's . . . something else . . . You know? Quite . . . differ— . . .'

'Ah yes, I see. Now Marie's pregnant and doing well, and that's great, isn't it?'

'But I won't be able to tell him.'

'Who?'

'The baby. I wanted to tell him stories like a . . . a . . . a . . . Oh, you said it just a minute ago.'

'A grandmother?'

'Yes.'

'And why won't you be able to tell him stories like a grandmother?'

'Too much . . . exhaust . . . and I'm so . . . tired. Aren't you?'

'No, I'm OK, Michka, I'm not tired. But it's fine if you are. You've done a lot of talking today. But you've seemed a bit sad lately, am I right?'

'You know, the cleaning lady brought me choux . . .'

'Shoes?

'No . . .'

She touches thumb to index finger and looks at me with a little hint of mischief through the hole this makes.

'Sweets?'

'No . . . in the shape of a . . . ring.'

'Choux buns?'

'That's it! Would you like one?'

'I wouldn't say no to a little one. And then we'll stop for today, OK?'

'And do you have any children?'

'Ah no, Michka. I'd have liked that, but I got divorced before I had any.'

'Really? And you haven't got a new one?'

I can't help laughing.

'You're very inquisitive, Michka! No, no "new one", to tell the truth.'

'Now, about your father . . .'

'Ah, that was a long time ago.'

We look at each other for a moment and I smile.

'I was thinking. Maybe you should . . . write . . . It would be a jest . . . a gesture.'

'I'll think about it, Michka. Why are you so bothered about this business with my father?'

'It's you.'

'What do you mean, it's me?'

'You're the one who's pothered.'

'No, no, come on. Don't worry. Did your medication get sorted out?'

'Yes, that's fine. They've . . . brought forward . . . my ten o'clock. That's fine.'

'Right, I'm going to let you rest. See you on Thursday, OK?'

I'm a speech therapist. I work with words and silence. The unsaid. I work with shame and secrets and regrets. I work with absence, vanished memories and the memories that resurface at the mention of a name, an image, a perfume. I work with old pain and pain that endures. Confidences.

And the fear of death.

That's part of my job.

What still surprises me, stuns me even, what can still take my breath away after ten years in the job, is how long childhood pain lasts. It leaves a burning, incandescent scar in spite of the years. It can't be erased.

I look at my old people. They're seventy, eighty, ninety. They tell me their distant memories. They talk about ancient, ancestral, prehistoric times. Their parents have been dead for fifteen, twenty, thirty years, but the pain of the child they once were is still there. Intact. You can see it clearly on their faces and hear it in their voices. I see it pulse in their bodies and their veins. A closed circuit.

When I arrive, I find her highly agitated. She's standing in the middle of the room on the verge of tears of rage. Her room's uncharacteristically untidy, as though she'd tried to move the furniture around but given up before she finished.

I knock and tiptoe in.

'Hello, Michka, how are you?'

'Nothing at all.'

'You seem angry?'

'It's the care assistant. She always appears from nowhere . . . Without knicking and she always wants to . . . eat everything.'

'The care assistant?'

'Yes.'

'She comes in without knocking?'

'Yes.'

'You need to speak to her, Michka. The same with the cleaner. And if she doesn't do as you ask, you should speak to the director.'

She sits down in her chair.

'But I can't say it, and so she doesn't understand. Even when I'm in the . . . the . . . she roils up just like that.'

'Do you want me to speak to her?'

'No, no, don't do that. She'll get angry. But what about you?' (She sizes me up.) 'You look sad.'

Old people are like children. You can't hide anything from them.

'Do you think so? No, everything's fine, I promise.'

'Speaking . . . is so diffu— . . . it's tiring, you know.'

'I understand, Michka.'

'The other day . . . I had a . . .' (She makes an odd gesture with one hand pointing to her head.) 'I'd like to tell you . . . but it's too far.'

'A dream?'

'Yes, but bad.'

'A nightmare?'

'Yes, with the . . . big cheese . . . She wanted me . . . vamoosed.'

'You've been anxious recently, Michka. Have you spoken to the care assistants?'

'No, I can't . . . show weakness to the officers . . . Definitely not.'

She walks round the room, then turns to me.

'I wanted to say . . .'

'Yes.'

'It's the . . . It's not what it was, you know. It's much less . . . and I forget the . . . So everything is . . . lest . . . lost . . . It makes me . . . fraid.'

'It makes you afraid?'

'Yes, but . . . also cold.'

'Has Marie been to see you?'

'No, that's over. She's . . .' (She holds her hand horizontal.) 'The doctor.'

'She has to stay in bed?'

'Yes.'

'For how long?'

'Full term.'

'Until the birth?'

'Yes.'

'Ah, that's a nuisance. But if it's for the good of the baby . . . And I'm sure she calls you often to give you news.'

'Yes, but I . . . I can't.'

'On the phone?'

'Yes, it's too far.'

'I understand. But that won't be for too much longer. Then Marie will be able to come and see you. Maybe even before the birth. Shall we do a little bit of work, if you're up for it?'

'All night.'

'I've brought some objects for a new exercise today. I want you to tell me what they're for and how you'd use them. All right?'

'All night.'

She looks at the things I take out of my bag with curiosity. One of them is a pad of writing paper that I put down in front of her.

'Ah, it's for . . . fetters . . . letters.'

'Very good. And? . . .'

'It's a . . . tad.'

'A pad, yes, which is used for . . .'

She makes a writing gesture but can't find the word.

I go on.

'For writing letters.'

'That's it.'

'Can you explain what you do?'

'You take a . . . then you open a . . .' (She mimes taking the top off a pen.) 'And there you are.'

'Perfect. Watch carefully. What do I do before I start writing?'

'You slide . . . the . . . lines . . .'

'Exactly, I slip the guide under the sheet so that I can write straight.'

'That's it.'

'Then, when you've finished the letter, what do you do?'

'You . . . slide it in.'

'In what?'

'The en— . . . entilope?'

'The envelope. And then you go to the . . . ?'

'Post office.'

'Very good.'

'What about you?'

'What *about* me?'

'Have you written your letter?'

'What letter, Michka?'

'To your father.'

'Well, you don't give up, I'll grant you that!'

She can't help looking a little pleased with herself. I smile.

'No, Michka, not yet. We'll see. In fact, shall we practise writing a few words today? I bet it's been ages since you did any writing too, Michka. You could write a few words to Marie on the pad. She'd like that, don't you think?'

'Yes, but . . . with a . . . that . . . Not that one.'

'Not that pen?'

'No. One that rubs out.'

'A pencil, you mean?'

'Yes.'

'I'm sure I've got one.'

I look in my bag and find a couple of pencils that I hand to her.

'And a rudder.'

'A rubber?'

'Yes.'

'Now, that I don't have.'

'I do. Go and look in the breadside . . .' (She points to her bedside table.)

'In the drawer?'

'That's right.'

'You want me to fetch a rubber from your drawer?'

'Yes, from the iron thing.'

I go to the bedside table while she's settling herself at the desk.

I open the drawer and find two old iron boxes, with a patina of age, the kind that junk-shop owners love. I open the first. It contains about fifty small yellow tablets. I'm taken by surprise and almost spill them everywhere. Michka hasn't noticed. My heart has started beating much faster. I open the second box, which contains, as expected, paper clips, staples and an eraser.

I take out the rubber, carefully closing the lid, and shut the drawer. She's leaning over the sheet of paper, trying to put down a few words in her trembling script, one hand resting on the paper, the other gripping the pencil.

I can't say anything. All those tablets in a box.

At least fifty, maybe more.

Saved up, without her carers knowing.

I remember the conversation she had with the nurse a few weeks ago.

So they're sleeping pills.

On the paper, Michka has written: 'Dear Marie'. Now she's waiting patiently, pencil poised.

She looks at me. She needs me for what comes next; she's intimidated by the blank page. I nod encouragingly. She's about to resume.

I go over.

I hesitate before saying anything.

'Michka, look at me.'

She raises her head like a child interrupted during dictation.

'Are you keeping your ten o'clocks?'

'What's that?'

Seeing her feigned innocence, I feel a strong desire to hug her.

'When I was looking for your rubber, I accidentally opened another metal box. You know what I saw, don't you, Michka?'

She hesitates for a moment. I know her, I know her well now. I sometimes even think I can read her mind.

'Wait. I'll tell you . . . It's just . . . to be . . . flee . . . you know?'

'To be free?'

'Yes. Free. That's it. Just to know. That it's fossible to . . . leave. While there's still time.'

We remain silent for a long time.

'You won't tell?'

'I need to think about it, Michka.'

Michka is standing opposite the nasty director, who is looking her up and down unsympathetically.

'Mrs Seld, it is with regret that I have to tell you we received a letter a few days ago from an informant who cites a number of very specific misdemeanours involving you and in addition notes all the official and unofficial items in your possession.'

'Really? Who could have done such a thing?'

'That doesn't matter. A neighbour, a visitor, a nurse, your friend Grace Kelly! Or perhaps even a care assistant enticed by your fan or your transistor! That's how the human soul is, Mrs Seld, and I doubt, given your origins, you're unaware of that. You don't really think things have changed? People will do anything for some furniture or a room with a view.'

'I don't have much, you know. I sold my apartment to pay the fees here. I've only one ring left and my transistor isn't worth tuppence ha'penny.'

'That's what you say. That's what they all say. And then you find the hoard. But that's beside the point. I think you know very well what we need to talk about.'

'Is this about the whisky?'

'Don't act the innocent, I beg you.'

'I don't understand.'

'Really? Are you sure? Shouldn't I alert the higher authorities of old age and funeral-insurance services about what's in your drawer, Mrs Seld? Your bedside-table drawer.'

Michka says nothing. Caught red-handed.

The director's tone becomes icy.

'Do you think you can just drop everything like that? Abandon your post, your duties? Do you think you get to decide? I would never have imagined this from a woman like you. We took you on because we thought you were worthy of our establishment. Because we thought you were prepared to fight to the end. Because that is what we expect of our members: a bit of fight, persistence, stubbornness. We've always struggled with turnover. It's a profitability issue. I'm well aware of what you're plotting, don't take me for a fool. I know what's in your drawer and how you plan to use them. That's why you're keeping your whisky! A fine mix . . . It's shameful, that's what it is.'

'No! Well, perhaps . . . or perhaps not. But they're not for now.'

'Really? And why should I believe you?'

'Because I'm hopeful.'

'Hopeful of what?'

'Finding them. So that I can go.'

'You should have thought of that sooner!'

'But I couldn't.'

'What are you talking about?'

'It's complicated. But also very simple.'

Michka sits down. She's trying to gather her memories, she's no longer looking at the director. Soon, she's no longer talking to the other woman, she's talking to herself or someone who is no longer there.

'It was one of my mother's cousins who came to fetch me. I was ten and I'd never seen her before. During the war she'd managed to go and stay with friends in Switzerland. Everything had to be rebuilt. Out of the ashes and the pain. She adopted me because she had no choice. We lived down there. She told me my parents had died in the camps and that was all. She couldn't talk about it. She behaved as though none of that had ever existed. Perhaps out of shame. You can't imagine the shame. The sadness. She was alive and everyone else was dead. Later, I searched. I found traces of them. What they'd suffered, the places they'd passed through. Drancy, Auschwitz. But there were also the memories that came back more and more often, haunted me, even. Distant memories that didn't match anything I'd been told. As though that had never existed. Faces of people I didn't recognise that began to fade, the river we used to swim in, the little wood behind the house that was full of brambles, the huge basins the washing soaked in, all these images that had no story attached. It was like fiction, a dream I'd invented. I understood that questions would cause pain and would never get an answer. I accepted silence. The woman raised me out of a sense of duty. She didn't have much money, but she paid for my education. When I came of age, she went to live in Poland. Everyone there had died too, but she rediscovered the places of her childhood. I visited her several times. The last time, shortly before she died, she finally told me. She told me about the young couple, Nicole and Henri, who risked their lives to save mine. She wasn't entirely sure of their first names, but for me they instantly resonated in a way that was intimate and familiar. She didn't know much about the three years I'd spent there. Only that they'd kept me close all that time and raised me as their own. After she died, I tried to find them. But I didn't know their surname. She'd forgotten it.'

The nasty director is pacing back and forth, waiting for Michka to finish her story, which she clearly finds of scant interest.

'But we won't make a fuss about it.'

'You don't understand.'

'I understand very well, Mrs Seld. You feel indebted and rude and you are not mistaken.'

'No, that's not it. It's something else. Something much bigger.'

'In any case, I've already told you, it's too late. You're not the first person to depart with a debt unsettled! But let me be quite clear on this: *when* you check out will be my decision.'

Ageing is growing used to loss.

Dealing almost each week with some new debit, some new deterioration, some new damage. That's what I see.

And nothing in the profit column any more.

One day no longer being able to run, walk, lean over, bend down, get up, reach, stretch, turn this way or that, neither forward nor back, not in the morning nor in the evening, not at all. Always having to adapt.

Losing your memory, losing your bearings, losing your words. Losing your balance, your sight, your sense of time, losing sleep, losing your hearing, losing the plot.

Losing what you've been given, what you've earned, what you've deserved, what you've fought for, what you thought was yours forever.

Readjusting.

Reorganising.
Doing without.
Just keeping going.
Having nothing left to lose.

It begins with small things. And then speeds up.

Because once they reach this stage, they're losing big time. Loads.

They lose the lot.

And they know that despite their efforts – the battle that starts again from square one every day – despite the goodwill they show, there's no escaping what's coming to them.

I knocked on the door, but she didn't answer.

I checked the corridor, thinking that she might not have come back from lunch. I asked the care assistants where she was. They were certain they'd seen her return to her room.

I go back and knock again. Still no answer, so I open the door and go in cautiously. She's sitting in her armchair staring into space. Her face looks thinner. She turns to me and smiles. It's been ages since I saw her. She's been ill and we've had to cancel several sessions. It only takes me a few seconds to realise she's given up.

A kick in the stomach wouldn't have hurt more. I don't know why it's so painful. I'm close to tears.

'Hello, Michka, how are you?'

She gives me another smile but doesn't answer.

'Are you tired?'

She nods almost imperceptibly.

'I can come back another time if you prefer.'

She looks at me but doesn't answer.

'Do you want me to stay awhile?'

'Yes.'

I take the chair and go nearer.

'I wanted to tell you . . . It's . . .'

She mimes something escaping or evaporating in front of her. This gesture of powerlessness really gets to me.

'It's all . . .'

'No, Michka, it's not all gone. You're feeling exhausted at the moment, that happens, but you need to get some rest and then we can get back to work again.'

'Oh no, I . . . But if you could . . .'

'I'll stay with you for a bit, don't worry. Has Marie phoned?'

'Yes, but . . .'

The same gesture of powerlessness.

'I . . . can't . . . so . . . I must . . .'

'Did she give you news?'

'Yes. She . . . tel— . . . but I can't . . . now . . . too much . . . and since . . . I always . . . it's so diffu— . . . diffuse.'

She looks at me guiltily.

'Don't worry, Michka, it'll be all right.'

Silence descends.

I could suggest a game or get my laptop out of my bag and show her pictures or play some music. Songs that were popular when she was a girl. That works well as a memory stimulus. The residents love it.

But I say nothing.

Sometimes you need to acknowledge the void left by the loss. Abandon distractions. Accept there's nothing more to say.

Stay sitting beside her. Take her hand.

We remain like that. She shuts her eyes. I lose track of time.

I feel her palm grow warmer in mine.

I think I can see a wave of wellbeing on her face.

A few minutes later, I get up.

'I'll come and see you again tomorrow, Michka.'

Just as I'm about to close the door behind me, she calls me back.

'Jérôme?'

It's unusual for her to use my first name. Most of the time she can't remember it.

'Yes?'

'Tank you.'

I see them as though I were there, in those empty, arid expanses, ruined pathways that suddenly appear in the middle of her sentences when she tries to speak. Desolate landscapes, devoid of light, unremittingly flat, and nothing, nothing at all to hold on to any more. Views of the end of the world. She begins a sentence and already words fail her; she lurches as if falling into a hole. There are no signposts or landmarks, because no path can cross this virgin terrain. The words have vanished and no picture will help get around that. Her voice, choked in the grip of defeat, is disintegrating. Unidentifiable obstacles block her way. Dark masses, themselves unnameable. Nothing can be shared any more. And each of her attempts falls into a bottom-less well from which nothing will ever be retrieved. She looks to me for a clue, a key, a way around. But my eyes can offer no help, no detour. The road is blocked.

Communication is cut.

Silence has won. And there's nothing left to hold her back.

MARIE

I haven't called to forewarn her. Telephone conversations have become so patchy and disorientating that they always leave me with an aftertaste of failure.

I go into the room quietly to give her time to adjust.

She's standing by the window as though I've caught her in a moment of uncertainty, of hesitation, frozen amid no man's land, between the armchair and the bed. What strikes me, shocks me even, is how much she's changed in just a few weeks.

She's *old*.

Now it's here.

Her face is lined, her skin has lost its colour, her body has shrunk, her balance seems more unsteady. I can't let her see the pain this image causes me. I mustn't appear surprised or afraid. My body mustn't betray me by wincing even a little. I keep smiling and go towards her.

She looks at me, incredulous. She can't get over it.

I can only guess the path this information must be taking to reach her brain, despite the lack of forewarning: it really is me coming towards her.

'Oh my, Marie . . . what about the doctor?'

She's impressed by the size of my stomach. Moved even.

We kiss. She stands by the foot of the bed so as not to wobble.

'Listen, I spend my time lying down at home from morning to night, I'll end up going crazy, so I decided to escape! I wanted to see you.'

'Was it . . . the . . . young . . . Jé— . . . The boy who told you?'

'Yes, Jérôme Milloux phoned. He told me he was taking a week off and thought you'd been a bit down lately, so he was worried about going off and you not having any visitors for a week, because Mrs Danville has flu. Did you know?'

'Ah . . . but he didn't . . . It isn't . . . all the same . . . you must . . . take care.'

'Sit down, Michka. I'll stay for a bit. And I need to sit down too. Don't worry. I came by taxi and I'll take one home. The baby's out of danger from this week, even if I give birth early.'

She sits down.

'Ah, that's better.'

I look at her. We're both feeling emotional.

'I'm so pleased to see you, Michk'!'

'Me too. Same.'

'You're not too bored?'

'A little . . . but not so much as such.'

'You know, I thought that as you can't read any more, I could bring you a CD player and some audiobooks. They do some great things.'

'No . . . no . . . it's too diffu— . . .'

'What's difficult? Listening to CDs?'

'No . . . the . . . the . . . machine.'

'The CD player? No, you'll see, it's not that complicated. I've got an old one with big buttons and everything's marked on them. I'll bring it next time.'

'All night . . . if you like.'

We sit in silence for a moment. She looks at me. She's smiling, but I can tell: she's given up. She's given up describing, explaining. She's pleased just to be able to pass the ball back.

'I don't know if I told you, but I've found a brilliant midwife at the hospital. She's looking after me.'

'Ah, good.'

'And my boss rang yesterday to see how I was doing and he was quite nice about everything. Even though I stopped work earlier than planned, he doesn't seem too put out.'

'And the . . .' (She's searching for a word and her hand indicates something big, bigger than her.) 'The Indian . . .'

'Lucas?'

'Yes, that's it.'

'Well, he's off next week. They brought his departure forward. The guy who had the job in India's moving on earlier than planned. So he won't even see the baby before he goes.'

'Ah . . . but . . . now?'

'He's very busy with work, preparing to leave and everything. But he's helped me all the same. He does my shopping for me, as I can't get around, and he's come to the hospital with me several times. But it's OK, Michk', you know. I'm coping. And anyway . . . I knew that when I made my decision. It'll be OK.'

Silence again.

I put my hands on my stomach on top of my dress.

'Is he moving?'

'Yes, he's moving. It's crazy.'

'It's a big one.'

'You're right. And he's beginning to weigh me down! At night it's hard to find a comfortable position. I toss and turn for hours. What about you, Michk', are you sleeping well?'

'Yes . . . it's fine.'

I have to get used to it. This silence.

'And what about Armande? How's she?'

'She was . . . in flu . . . too. In the . . . haven't . . . seen.'

'So she's stayed in her room?'

'Yes. Still . . . there.'

'Poor Michk', the days must feel long.'

'Not so much as such. But . . . I'm no good.'

'What about the TV?'

'Oh no, you know . . . too noisy.'

'I saw a film the other day that Lucas downloaded onto my computer. I watched it at home on my own, lying quietly on the sofa. But when the film ended, I cried and cried! You can't imagine . . . I couldn't stop.'

'Oh . . . it's because you're . . . inspecting . . . maybe.'

'No, no. Well, maybe, but not just that. Shall I tell you the story?'

Finally, there's a spark in her eye. She loves me telling her stories from films and books and my friends' lives. She's listening with the special attention she reserves for stories.

'It's about this young boy – he's twelve or thirteen – who's being brought up by his father. It's set in Belgium, in quite a poor part that's going through hard times. You realise the boy's mother's gone, but don't know why. The father's gone back to live with *his* mother, the boy's grandmother, and his two brothers. They're all out of work. They've nothing to do all day but drink. It's not really sad, there are even some very happy times. They go for bike rides, watch TV. But the father regularly hits the boy. Perhaps because he feels his son's growing away from him or there's something different about him. One day a social worker comes to the house. The father goes crazy and hits the grandmother because he thinks she told social services. The grandmother keeps quiet. The boy's sent off to a home. He starts to read, to study. He begins a new life. Later it turns out he's become a writer. He's living with a woman who's going to have a baby. Near the end there's a great moment where he goes to visit his grandmother, who's in a retirement home. He goes to say thank you. He thanks her for not giving him away, for not telling his father it wasn't her who contacted the social worker. It was him. You can't imagine how much I cried. It's a really beautiful film about the way things begin, about how people move on from where they start out. You'd have liked it, Michka, for sure.'

She suddenly looks pensive.

'Ah yes . . . yes.'

'And I want to say thank you too, Michka. Thank you for everything. Without you, I don't know what would have become of me. Without you, I wouldn't have been able to stay in rue des Amandiers. Without you, I maybe wouldn't have found shelter. And later I wouldn't have been able to study, and then, when I was ill, you were there too, you know, and I don't know if I would have been able to . . . get myself back together. Without you.'

Michka's trying to hide how emotional she's feeling; she's hunting in her trouser pocket in the hope of finding a tissue.

'Oh . . . no.'

'Oh yes.'

'You . . . you always . . . exagitate.'

We're quiet for a moment.

'What's it called?'

'The film?'

'Yes.'

'*Merditude.*'

'Ah . . . *Mercitude* . . .'

She ponders for a moment, suddenly very serious.

'That's a nice . . . fine word . . . But are you sure it's real?'

It's grown dark. The floral curtains are drawn.

Michka is standing under the yellow overhead light. Alone in the middle of her room, she goes through a sequence of silent movements. Cautiously at first, and then more confidently.

She's dancing.

She raises her arms, spins around. Bends forward in a sort of bow, then straightens up proudly.

She almost loses her balance several times, but always manages to regain it.

The little girl's voice returns, as though in a dream.

Am I going to sleep at yours? Will you leave the light on? Will you stay here? Can you leave the door open? Will you stay with me? Can we have breakfast together? Are you scared? Do you know where my school is? Don't put the light out, OK? Will you take me if Mummy can't?

Michka opens her arms, then wraps them around her body, with her palms flat against her back. She hugs herself for a moment, as though trying to hold on to someone, as though she were cradling a child.

The real director knocks and enters the room. Michka's in bed.

'Hello, Mrs Seld, how are you?'

'I'm fine.'

'Mr Milloux, your speech therapist, is on holiday this week, do you remember?'

'Yes, definitely.'

'He called me this morning to ask me to pass on a message. He told me it was very important. As you can no longer use the phone, he gave it to me.'

She takes a piece of paper from her pocket on which she's jotted down a few words so that she wouldn't forget anything.

'He says to tell you he's found the people. The people from La Ferté-sous-Jouarre you were looking for. They don't live there any more, but they're in the area. He's going to see the lady – she's still alive. He'll tell you about it all.'

Michka needs a moment to absorb this information.

'Is this . . . serious?'

'Yes, of course, Mrs Seld. Entirely serious.'

'Oh, tank you. Tank you so much.'

Michka thinks for a moment.

'We need to say . . . to Marie. He . . . he . . .'

'Tell her?'

'Yes.'

'I'll see to it, Mrs Seld. I'll ring her and give her Mr Milloux's message, word for word. That's what you want, isn't it? All right?'

'Yes, all night.'

'And I also wanted to tell you I spoke to the care assistant and explained things to her. She's promised to be careful and not to redo things you've already done. She's off at the moment, but she'll be back next week and I'll come and see you to check how things are going.'

'I don't know how to . . .'

'Don't thank me, Mrs Seld, it's my job. I must get on. Have a good day.'

JÉRÔME

She's waiting for me determinedly.

She knows my timetable. She knows I'm in the building from the morning, though our appointment's not till three. Like every Tuesday. She's probably wondering if I'll drop in to see her before that, pop my head round the door, just for a quick chat. I thought about it but was afraid it would agitate her needlessly. I need time to tell her all about it.

———

It's three o'clock when I eventually go into her room.

She's made an effort to get up (the staff have told me that recently she's been spending her days in bed).

She's dressed and is wearing the floral scarf that I've complimented her on several times. She's sitting in her armchair.

When she sees me, her face lights up.

'Ah! Hello . . . Jé— . . .'

'Hello, Michka, I'm really pleased to see you. I've missed you, you know.'

She smiles. Readjusts what remains of her hairstyle.

'How do you feel?'

'Fine, fine. So what about . . . the . . . friends?'

'Ah, I've lots to tell you. Are you ready?'

'Oh yes, very.'

Her face is turned towards me.

It's as though everything has slowed down: her heart-beat, the speed of her movements, the blinking of her eyes. The room is pure silence.

'I'll tell you about it from the beginning. You know I called Marie before I left? I thought you seemed very tired. I was worried about you. We talked for a bit. She told me you were looking for the people who'd saved you during the war and that you'd put another ad in but hadn't had a response. She told me what she knew. She realised it was making you sad. I had no particular plans for my holiday, so I decided to go there. To La Ferté-sous-Jouarre. I like doing things on the spur of the moment. I found a very nice little hotel and hung around for a couple of days, asking questions in cafés, bakeries, at the lawyer's and the doctor's. Eventually I found an old cobbler who'd known Nicole and Henri Olfinger. The first names matched and there'd been a rumour they'd hidden a little Jewish girl for several years. The cobbler gave me the name of their daughter,

Madeleine, who got married and still lives in La Ferté. I went to see her. She was very welcoming and confirmed the story. Her parents often used to tell her it. So they were still thinking about you.'

I pause to see if she's holding up. Her eyes are fixed on me. She's waiting for me to go on.

'It was your mum who took you. She wanted to get you into the free zone and leave you with some friends of your parents near Lyons. But the railway line had been bombed and the train stopped in open country not far from La Ferté-sous-Jouarre. Your mother took your hand and you walked for ages. And then she saw the first house, a kilometre outside town. She told you to wait by a tree and not move. She went and knocked. Nicole Olfinger came to the door. Your mum begged this woman she'd never met before to take in her seven-year-old daughter. She said, "You have to take the little one. I'll come back, but you have to take her from me today. Please." Henri came to the door, they looked at each other and then said yes. Your mother repeated that she'd come back. But she never did.'

I pause again. I look at Michka. Her face gives nothing away beyond her intense concentration on my story.

'They were well aware of what they were doing. Of the risks. They burned your coat with the yellow star sewn onto it. They hid you. All that time. They told friends and neighbours you were their niece. In October 1943, there was a round-up in La Ferté-sous-Jouarre and about fifteen people were deported. Nicole and Henri

129

were afraid of being denounced. They hid you in the barn under a tarpaulin for a whole night, but no one came. Later, when the war was over, a woman turned up at the door one morning. Your mother's cousin. Your mother had written her a letter with a plan drawn from memory to explain where she'd left you. In case things went wrong. Your parents were deported a few days after she got back from La Ferté. That's the story I was told by Madeleine, Nicole and Henri Olfinger's daughter, who was born after the war. Your story. When they took you in, they'd just got married. Henri died a few years ago, but Nicole's still there. She lives locally in a retirement home. She's ninety-nine.'

Michka is sitting across from me. Tears are flowing silently down her cheeks.

I take her hands. They're so cold I fear that her heart has stopped.

'Are you OK? Do you want me to go on?'

She nods.

'I went to see Nicole Olfinger. She's blind and has trouble hearing. But she's got all her marbles. I told her about you. I told her you'd looked for them, but you didn't know their surname. She understood. I took the liberty of telling her how important it was to you, now, to be able to express your gratitude. She was deeply moved, you know. I told her how happy you'd be to know she was still alive. To know it wasn't too late. When I asked her how they'd kept going during those three years, she said something I wanted to be sure to

130

pass on to you: "You reject the worst option. And after that, your choice is made." She also said: "There's no point being big-headed about things like that."'

Michka's now hiding her face in her hands.

'You know, Michka, I cried too when I left that room.'

She remains like that for a few minutes.

'It's a lot of emotions all at once, isn't it?'

She doesn't answer. But I hear her breathing and can tell how determined she is to hold back the sobs.

'In the spring we could maybe take you there, who knows?'

She lowers her hands and looks at me.

'Yes . . . but . . . I'm so . . . zausted. Maybe.'

'If you like, I can come back tomorrow with my pad of writing paper and help you write a letter. OK?'

Her chin is trembling, but the tears have stopped.

'All night.'

The next day I find her at her desk.

Ready.

I sit down beside her.

I slide the pad in front of her and give her one of my pencils. She doesn't like ballpoints or felt tips. She wants to be able to rub out, to start again. For a few minutes she sits, pencil poised. Waiting for the words.

I know how rare they are now. Distant, buried, scrambled.

'Do you want me to help you, Michka?'

She indicates she doesn't.

I back off.

I sit at the foot of her bed and look out the window.

We have plenty of time.

I see she's writing. Very slowly. A dozen words or so. Her hand's shaking, but she sticks at it. I know that at this moment she's giving her all, everything she has left. She's using her final reserves.

I hear the sound of pencil on paper. Pressing hard.

I almost want to stretch out on the bed and go to sleep for a little while.

Because in this room, near this old lady, I feel strangely secure.

She has finished.

She folds the paper.

Without looking, I slip the sheet into the envelope and she watches me seal it. She has the right to that dignity, after all. I write the name of Nicole Olfinger's retirement home and her room number.

'I'll post it when I leave.'

She nods.

'Shall I see you on Thursday?'

She nods again, exhausted.

But just before I go, she beckons me back.

'And you? . . . Your f— . . . father?'

'Ah.'

'What to do?'

'I don't know, Michka.'

'But why such a long time?'

'You know, my father's never really tried to see me again. In fact, I think he finds my presence unbearable. He doesn't know me. All he has is a false, distorted image of me that he's fixed for all eternity.'

'But why?'

'I don't know. Maybe just because I'm not the son he dreamed of. As if something about me offended him. He saw me as the enemy. He'd seek out the proof of that, my shortcomings. And then retaliate in his own way. But words do harm, you know. Insults, sarcasm, criticism, reproaches leave their mark. Indelibly. And that judgemental look, seeking a weakness. And then there were the threats. Things like that leave an impression, you know. It's hard to have trust after that. To feel any love for yourself. He's suffered. A lot. I know that. And time's going by, it's true, you're right about that. But does there come a point when things calm down? I don't know. I'm not sure. I'd like to believe it. I forgave him a long time ago. But I don't know if something else is possible. Something kinder.'

Her eyes are still on me.

By way of reply, she hands me the pad and the pencil I lent her.

'All that. Put it down.'

'Put it down where, Michka?'

'On paper.'

'OK, I promise. I'll put it all down on paper.'

She and I are face to face.

'So, Michka, you strike me as being on top form today. Shall we do a little exercise to warm up? Give me ten words that rhyme with "home".'

She fires back: 'Dome, comb, tome, chrome, loam, gnome, foam, roam, gastronome, catacomb.'

'Amazing! I can tell you're an expert. And now, words that rhyme with . . .'

'End.'

'Ah . . . OK . . . If you like.'

'No, your turn.'

'OK then . . . send, bend, trend.'

'Is that all?'

She loves to tease me.

'I'll help you: spend, lend, penned, wend, blend, friend . . . mend.'

'Bravo, Michka. You're better than me at this!'

I let the silence settle on us; it's a space you have to know how to share.

But after a moment I can't stop myself saying, 'I hate it, Michka, I'll be frank, when people leave without warning.'

'I don't know what you mean.'

'We should have forewarning. When people are going to die. Whether it's their choice or not, I don't care – after all, that's up to them. But you should get a letter or a text or a voicemail, an email, or something, something very clear and unambiguous: "Please note, Mr So-and-So, Mrs Such-and-Such, your cousin, friend, husband, neighbour, mother is likely to disappear in the near, or very near, future." Shit.'

I'm getting worked up needlessly. It seems to have made an impression on Michka. So I try to explain.

'It's true, it's painful at the end. You always think you have time to say things and then suddenly it's too late. You think that showing, signalling is enough, but it's not. You have to say it. *Say*, that word that you like so much. Words count. I don't need to tell you that. You were a proofreader for a big publisher, I believe.'

'What would you like to say?'

'I don't know! Two or three things for the road . . . "That was nice", "Delighted to have met you", "Honoured", "Enchanted", "Have a safe journey", "All the best as you venture into the unknown", "Thanks for everything" – I don't know! Or perhaps just . . . a hug.'

'Please do.'

I approach her. I feel her frail body leaning into mine, carefully at first, then she gives herself to the embrace.

Suddenly Jacques Brel's voice fills her small room.

We trace some dance steps.

A waltz in hundred time
A waltz when you're a hundred
A waltz that's heard
At every crossroads
In Paris, which love
Renews in springtime

She breaks away first.

'You're dreaming, Jérôme, don't you think? Well, to tell the truth, I don't know if it's me who's dreaming or you! But I'm sure this is a dream.'

JÉRÔME (2)

I liked her immediately.

I recognised her, yes, that's the right word.

I thought: I'll take everything.

The smile, the sadness, the dark eyes.

The little girl who went out in the park with no coat.

The young woman with the big belly bulging out of her coat.

The baby, the bathwater, the steam on the mirror.

MARIE

There are all the trite, hand-me-down words people use in these situations.

To console others. To try to lessen their pain. And our own at the same time.

'You did all you could', 'You were really important to her', 'It's lucky you were there', 'She was really fond of you', 'She spoke of you often.'

No one will ever contradict you.

This morning when the alarm went off, Michka didn't open her eyes.

She died in her sleep.

It's the best death she could have hoped for. I know that.

Before she lost everything.

I meet Jérôme in the corridor.

He seems very upset.

'Hi, I'm Jérôme.'

'Hi, I'm Marie.'

'I'd rather have met you in . . . other circumstances. Have you been able to see her?'

'Yes, I spent the morning by her side. Before they took her away. She looked at peace. Her face was calm. It was as if she'd fallen asleep like that, safe in the knowledge that she wouldn't wake up again.'

For a moment, he won't meet my eye; he's looking into the distance at some dark thought. And then his eyes again.

'Did they find anything in particular? I mean . . . did the doctor tell you anything?'

'No. Nothing else. She died in her sleep. She didn't suffer. It's what we all hope for, isn't it?'

'Yes, absolutely.'

He's watching me, hesitating for a moment.

'And what about you, Marie, how're you? Things not too . . . diffu—?'

I smile.

'They're tough . . . but not so much as such.'

Then he smiles.

'I wanted to give you a big tanks, Jérôme. If you'll allow me to call you Jérôme. For everything you did for her. I sometimes thought about going down there. But

I didn't dare. I was afraid it would be too emotional for her, she wouldn't have the strength. But you were right.'

'You know, she gave me a lot. A huge amount. I don't know why you feel closer to some patients than others. But I should have said tank you to her too.'

'I think you did it in your own way. Will you come to the cremotion?'

'Yes, all night.'

'There'll be little sandwiches.'

'With salami, I hope!'

'I'll make sure. And spammon.'

'And if you need help clearing the room, don't hesitate to call me. I'm often in this neck of the woods, you know.'

'Thank you.'

'So, see you soon?'

'Yes, see you soon.'

I watch him walk off down the corridor. He goes into another room.

I hear his clear voice through the door.

'So, Mrs Lefébur, how are you today?'

ALSO AVAILABLE BY DELPHINE DE VIGAN

LOYALTIES

'Narrated with punch and pace. You're kept reading helplessly to the desperate cliffhanger finish'
Daily Mail

Thirteen-year-old Théo and his friend Mathis have a secret.

Their teacher, Hélène, suspects something is not right with Théo and becomes obsessed with rescuing him, casting aside her professionalism to the point of no return.

Cécile, mother of Mathis, discovers something horrifying on her husband's computer that makes her question whether she has ever truly known him.

Respectable facades are peeled away as the four stories wind tighter and tighter together, pulling into a lean and darkly gripping novel of loneliness, lies and loyalties.

'Delphine de Vigan's dark family thrillers are a cult sensation ... A powerful exploration of neglect'
i paper

'Taut and fascinating'
Guardian

'A taut, intense novel of secrets, lies and the unknowable depths of others'
Tatler

BASED ON A TRUE STORY

'A wonderful literary trompe l'oeil: a book about friendship, writing and the boundary between reality and fantasy ... Dark, smart, strange, compelling'
Harriet Lane, bestselling author of *Her*

Overwhelmed by the huge success of her latest novel, exhausted and unable to begin writing her next book, Delphine meets L.

L. is the kind of impeccable, sophisticated woman who fascinates Delphine; a woman with smooth hair and perfectly filed nails, and a gift for saying the right thing. Delphine finds herself irresistibly drawn to her, their friendship growing as their meetings, notes and texts increase. But as L. begins to dress like Delphine, and, in the face of Delphine's crippling inability to write, L. even offers to answer her emails, and their relationship rapidly intensifies. L. becomes more and more involved in Delphine's life until she patiently takes control and turns it upside down: slowly, surely, insidiously.

'Combining the allure of *Gone Girl* with the sophistication of literary fiction, *Based on a True Story* is a creepy but unapologetically clever psychological thriller'
Independent

'The latest literary sensation ... It has people in a word-of-mouth frenzy I've not seen since *Gone Girl* ... De Vigan's description of a close female friendship is a compulsive but agonising read'
Daily Telegraph

'This is that rare beast – a fine thriller and a potential literary sensation. Patricia Highsmith would have been proud. Don't miss it'
Daily Mail

BLOOMSBURY

UNDERGROUND TIME

'One of those books that grabs you and demands to be read'
Clare Morrall

Every day Mathilde takes the Metro to the office of a large multinational, where she works in the marketing department. And every day Thibault, a paramedic, drives to the addresses he receives from his controller. Mathilde is unhappy at work, frozen out of office life by her moody boss. Meanwhile, Thibault is unhappy in love and all too aware that he may be the only human being many of the people he visits will see for the entire day. Mathilde and Thibault seem to be just two anonymous figures in a crowded city, pushed and shoved and pressured continuously by the isolating urban world. But surely these two complementary souls, travelling their separate tracks, must meet?

'Delphine de Vigan is a sensation'
Observer

'What's most startling about this novel is how de Vigan makes the mundane come alive. She's an expert in detail, charging even the most ordinary situation with emotion, which makes for a massively affecting read'
Psychologies

'Sympathetic, compelling, enjoyable'
Guardian

ORDER YOUR COPY:

BY PHONE: +44 (0) 1256 302 699
BY EMAIL: DIRECT@MACMILLAN.CO.UK
DELIVERY IS USUALLY 3–5 WORKING DAYS.
FREE POSTAGE AND PACKAGING FOR ORDERS OVER £20.
ONLINE: WWW.BLOOMSBURY.COM/BOOKSHOP
PRICES AND AVAILABILITY SUBJECT TO CHANGE WITHOUT NOTICE.

WWW.BLOOMSBURY.COM/DELPHINE-DE-VIGAN

BLOOMSBURY

NOTHING HOLDS BACK THE NIGHT

'Delphine de Vigan is a sensation'
Observer

In this moving autobiographical novel, the narrator's mother, Lucile, raises her two daughters largely alone. A former child model from a large Bohemian family, Lucile is younger and more glamorous than the other mothers: always in lipstick and stylishly dressed, wayward and wonderful. But as the years pass her occasional sadness gives way to overwhelming despair and delusion.

This is a story of luminous beauty and rambunctious joy, of dark secrets and silences, revelations and, ultimately, the unknowability of even those closest to us. And in the face of the unknowable, personal history becomes fiction. *Nothing Holds Back the Night* is universally recognisable and singularly heartbreaking.

'The only way to read this book is to stop, put it down, gasp, absorb the horrors and then read on'
Eileen Battersby, *Irish Times*

'Thrilling, tender ... A genuinely shocking, incandescent read'
Scotland on Sunday

'Compassionate and powerful, as well as painful and shocking ... The luminous accuracy of the prose reminds me of Colette ... Overflowing with life and vibrant personalities, almost enough to conceal the lurking darkness'
Ursula K. Le Guin, *Guardian*

BLOOMSBURY

NO AND ME

A Richard & Judy Book Club selection

Thirteen-year-old Lou Bertignac's has an IQ of 160, a mother who barely speaks and hasn't left the house in years, and a father who is struggling to keep his family together. But then she meets and gradually befriends No, a homeless girl a few years older than herself. As the two girls learn to trust each other, Lou resolves to help her new friend build a stable life for herself, unaware that No's sudden presence will soon change her family forever.

'This novel is a thing of poetic beauty'
The Times

'Moments of tenderness and truth about family and home'
Independent on Sunday

'Well-structured, with moments of tenderness and truth about family and home, inadequate parents and neglected children'
Independent

BLOOMSBURY

A Note on the Type

The text of this book is set in Adobe Garamond. It is one of several versions of Garamond based on the designs of Claude Garamond. It is thought that Garamond based his font on Bembo, cut in 1495 by Francesco Griffo in collaboration with the Italian printer Aldus Manutius. Garamond types were first used in books printed in Paris around 1532. Many of the present-day versions of this type are based on the *Typi Academiae* of Jean Jannon cut in Sedan in 1615.

Claude Garamond was born in Paris in 1480. He learned how to cut type from his father and by the age of fifteen he was able to fashion steel punches the size of a pica with great precision. At the age of sixty he was commissioned by King Francis I to design a Greek alphabet, and for this he was given the honourable title of royal type founder. He died in 1561.